The Children
of
Battleship Row

Pearl Harbor 1940–1941

The Children
of
Battleship Row

Pearl Harbor 1940–1941

Joan Zuber Earle

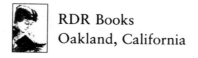
RDR Books
Oakland, California

The Children of Battleship Row: Pearl Harbor 1940 - 1941

RDR Books
4456 Piedmont Avenue
Oakland, California 94611
Phone: (510) 595-0595
Fax: (510) 595-0598
E-mail: read@rdrbooks.com
Website: www.rdrbooks.com

ISBN: 1 - 57143 - 095 - 4
Library of Congress Catalog Card Number: 2001098533

Editor: Helen J. Harris
Cover Design: Richard K. Harris

Photographs used with permission:
Zuber Family, *Z*
National Archives, *NA*
U. S. Naval Institute, Annapolis, MD, *USNI*
Pearl Harbor Library, *PHL*
Sherman Grinberg Film Library, Newsreel: *Refugees from Pearl Harbor*, *SGFL*
(Numbers begin with cover photos)
NA: 5, 15, 18, 19, 20, 22
USNI: 2, 14, 16, 17, 21, 23, 24
SGFL: 25, 26, 27
Z: 1, 3, 4, 6, 7, 8, 9, 10, 11, 12, 13, 28, 29, 30, 31

LITTLE BROWN GAL
By Lee Wood, Don Dairmid and Johnny Noble
Copyright 1935 by Bourne Co.
Copyright renewed
All Rights Reserved International Copyright Secured

Distributed in Canada by Starbooks c/o Fraser Direct
100 Armstrrong Avenue, Georgetown, Ontario. L7G 5S4

Distributed in England and Europe by Airlift Book Company,
8 The Arena, Mollison Avenue, Enfield, Middlesex, England EN37NJ

Second Printing

Printed in Canada by Transcontinental

For the children of Pearl Harbor,
and all children of war

Prologue

December 1991

The ferry that moves quietly away from its slip and begins plying across the harbor toward Ford Island is not the familiar red and white checkerboard one of the past. And even this ferry will become just another memory when they complete the bridge currently under consideration.

I stand alone on the lower deck, my hands gripping the rail, my face buffeted by the warm wind. I block out all sounds, for I'm lost in memories of that October day more than fifty years ago when I first saw the island.

I close my eyes, hearing again John Phillips Souza floating over from a band on a ship now buried at sea. Phantom ship's bells again toll the time. In memory's eye, small boats and launches cross the seemingly-carefree harbor to and from the huge ships of our fleet gallantly moored at their stations. We are passing by the Admiral's pier next, turning down the now-empty row, our passage witnessed only by the silent white Memorial. I look sharply to the left of the Memorial. There! Resting on the crest of the embankment facing the harbor stands Quarters T, unchanged amidst all changes.

We pass the small launch ramp with its arching algarroba tree. The site of my beloved Kenneth Whiting School is an empty grass field, but I can hear the echo of

1

children's voices singing, laughing. We ease into the island slip with the same familiar bumps and thumps as in the past.

It is the time of returning, of coming home to a place I loved so well and lost so suddenly.

One

1940

One September evening, a Marine Corporal rang the doorbell at our quarters on the United States Naval Air Station, San Diego, California. My father, Major Adolph Zuber, U.S.M.C., was Commanding Officer, Post Quartermaster, Post Exchange and NAS Athletic Officer. The corporal saluted my father smartly and handed him a telegram.

I was eight years old and my sister, Peggy, was nine. Just two months earlier, we had arrived here with Daddy for a two-year term of duty. I liked the one-story Spanish style house with its palm trees and its close proximity to the Officers' Club swimming pool.

But I hated Coronado School. Mother admonished me, "Joan, never say hate. Say you dislike something intensely. Hate is too strong a word." But I hated this new school because they were not going to permit me to skip. The previous June I had been skipped a half year to the high fourth grade, but this school did not have half-year skips. They were making me take a test to see if I qualified to skip a whole year.

The afternoon the telegram arrived, I had sat at the scarred wooden desk with its individual inkwell, the teacher facing me. "How many pecks are there in a bushel?" the question asked. I didn't know. The answer was in the notebook on the shelf under my desk and I wanted to peek, but I couldn't. I felt I would be doomed to repeat everything I'd already learned and to stay in that school for the two years Daddy was stationed there.

Peggy had her own set of problems: she missed Janice Pritchard.

Marine Juniors -- that's what they called us -- do not have many friends. We'd already moved often and lived in many places: Washington D.C., Bremerton, Washington; Quantico, Virginia; the California cities of Long Beach and San Diego, as well as the island in San Francisco Bay. We always seemed to be saying goodbye. But Peggy had one special friend, Janice Pritchard, a girl with bright yellow blonde hair, someone we'd met in 1937 in San Diego while Daddy was in China.

I was one mad Marine on the afternoon of that September day when the Navy school bus dropped Peggy and me off. I walked into the quarters, threw my books on the floor, and announced, "I'm never going back to that school again."

Peggy brushed past my pile of books on her way to our bedroom, saying "Don't disturb me. I have to write and invite Janice to my birthday party in three weeks. I know she's in Hawaii, but I still want to ask her."

An uneasy silence reigned over the quarters: my books were still on the floor, Peggy was writing her letter, and Daddy arrived home for dinner. There was a strangeness around the table, where usually my parents talked about what was going on in Europe. I'd been marking the changing boundaries on the globe I'd purchased,

Or they'd discuss how the book they'd written together, *Let's All Play*, on enjoying the game of Bridge with an odd number of people, was selling in the local stores.

I tried to break the ice. "They're still going over multiplication. The only good place in that school is the library."

Mother retorted, "You may be excused from the table, Joan, and please pick up your books from the hall."

Peggy left the table, heading back to her room. "I've got to finish my letter." I was just about to leave, too.

And then the front doorbell rang and the corporal delivered the telegram.

We were worried. Had something happened to Daddy's East Coast relatives? The last telegram we'd received told of his father's death. Daddy opened the envelope and slowly read the message, a look of bewilderment on his face. He passed it to Mother.

She read it and grew very quiet. Daddy called Peggy from our room and read it to us: "You are ordered to report to the United States Naval Air Station, Ford Island, Pearl Harbor, assuming command of the Marine Barracks, October 16, 1940. Reservations have been made for your family to embark on the *Lurline*, October 10, 1940."

I screamed with joy: No more Coronado School! Peggy rushed back to our bedroom to rewrite her letter to Janice, inviting her to a birthday party now suddenly, miraculously, rescheduled in Hawaii.

But Mother was very, very quiet. Her face was white. Her voice shook as she said, determined, "I am not going to Pearl Harbor. You may go, but I am not going."

"We'll go without you," I answered. I had such a quiet voice, my mother sometimes called me "My angel, softly spoken."

It didn't matter what I or Peggy or Daddy said that night; we couldn't change her mind. She repeated the phrase all evening, "I will not go to Pearl Harbor."

I thought she'd change her mind by the next morning, but I was wrong. She didn't get out of bed, and we left on the school bus without her hug. I was still exultant; I could even smile at Billy, the boy who lived in the quarters next door and who'd called me "Four-eyes." The last time he'd called me "Four-eyes" I'd grabbed his thin blonde hair, pulled hard, and it had come out in my hand. Well, that was all in the past now. We were leaving.

"It's all about the furniture and the drapes," Peggy suggested on the bus. "She's been so excited about those swatches of fabrics for the furniture. This was the first time she'd ever been able to decorate a quarters, the first time she could plant flowers and watch them come up."

I agreed that she'd been happy, but somehow it seemed that it was more than redecorating or flowers. This time, something was really wrong.

Daddy was our hero, the son of an immigrant Swiss baker. He'd been born in Elizabeth, New Jersey, in 1902. Football and high grades had won Daddy a scholarship to Syracuse University where he'd wanted to study law. But there was no money, so he took the competitive examination for the United States Naval Academy and was accepted. He played center on their football team, travelling by train to Pasadena to play in the 1924 Rose Bowl, where Navy tied the University of Washington, fourteen to fourteen.

His stomach, however, had made him a Marine. Mother'd told us the story: "On his first cruise in 1921, he woke up in the morning and, vomiting violently, made his way to the deck to find out how far they were at sea. He was told they were still tied up at the dock."

At graduation he opted to be a Marine, where he would have less sea duty.

Mother, Alice Rita Brady, had been born in New York in 1908 and as a young woman had worked as a companion-secretary for Hattie Strong, a philanthropist and friend of education.

Our Great-aunt Peggy, Mother's only living relative, had brought my parents together initially in 1929. Married to Colonel Harold Utley, U.S.M.C., she'd gone against orders, taking her jewelry with her to Nicaragua. So she'd asked a young lieutenant stationed there to take it back to the states and deliver it at dockside, to her niece. My mother, a diminutive five foot two, entranced my six foot one father. They were married three months later in the Naval Academy Chapel.

We were true Marines. My sister, Peggy, had been inducted at the moment of her birth in Port-au-Prince, Haiti, October 18, 1930. My induction came fourteen months later, December 29, 1931, in the Washington, D.C. Naval Yard. We'd played "The Marine Corp Hymn" at our first piano recital, May 12, 1937, at the Officers' Club in Quantico, Virginia, where Daddy was then stationed. We'd had our inoculation shots and our stitches after accidents without a tear because Mother had always told us, "Marines don't cry." And we felt like Marines, proud of our father and our country.

Now we heard our parents' voices raised, night after night, my father cajoling my mother, "Alice, it's only an island. Ford Island in the middle of Pearl Harbor. You've been on islands before."

My mother would answer, "It's more than an island. It's *the* island." She would raise her voice when saying the phrase. Peggy and I, listening from our bedroom, couldn't understand.

Days passed. Time was getting short. I had an early morning job: to polish my father's shoes on his white wooden shoe shine box. It was something I liked to do. Finally one morning when my mother still was not hearing me, I tried writing down what I wanted her to hear. I used the Shinola dauber of brown liquid polish to print across the top of the box a note to Mother, "We want you to go."

The written message finally seemed to do it. She changed her mind. She ordered the furniture packers. And she took Peggy and me across on the ferry to buy clothes in San Diego. "You will need tropical clothes," she announced. Matching dresses of course -- Peggy and I were always dressed alike -- two dimity floral prints, hand-tucked on the bodice, and two dresses of pure coral with white scalloped insets down the front. Into the suitcases went the blue suspender skirts with matching capes that Mother had sewn for us, and the navy blue Panama hats. Mother packed up her dreams of redecorated quarters. She retrieved the copies of *Let's All Play* from the book stores. But her face was strained and her smile was gone.

What Peggy and I did not know was that in June of 1940 the War Department had sent the first attack alert to the Hawaii Army and Navy Command, cautioning them to avoid publicity and not in any way alert the news reporters. Nor did we realize that that same June, while our family was visiting my father's family in New Jersey, Daddy himself had predicted the attack. *The Daily Journal* of Elizabeth quoted his forecast that the Japanese would "probably strike suddenly as was the case when they began the Russo-Japanese war early in the century." My mother, of course, knew all of this.

We learned later that she had also had a dream that she was leading us, her daughters, into great danger.

Two

In1940, there were only two ways to travel to Hawaii: by Pan American Clipper or by ship. We were sailing on the pride of the Matson Line.

In Wilmington, California, we boarded a pristine white ship with a large navy blue M -- for Matson liner -- on her buff funnels, and her name proudly declared in large block letters on her bow, L U R L I N E. Bands played and the air was full of colorful paper serpentine streamers thrown from the ship to people on the dock below, streamers which seemed to tie the ship to the pier.

And then the ship began to move, parting the fragile paper strands. I held the sheared pieces tightly in my hands, watching the widening gulf between land and ship.

On the *Lurline*, I felt like Shirley Temple in my favorite movie, "The Little Princess." We were treated like royalty: paradise for an eight year old. Daddy had upgraded our tickets to B Deck, the Promenade Deck. Peggy and I shared a cabin with two twin beds, windows opening out on the promenade, and a telephone to call and order, "Lemonade to the room please."

We only had one important lesson to learn on the ship, lifeboat drills. At first Peggy and I were worried, but Mother said, "It's only in case of trouble." A voice on the loudspeaker would command us to put on our life jackets and proceed to our lifeboat, where everyone laughed as we went through the drill.

While Mother and Daddy entered the bridge tournament, Peggy and I roamed the ship, tasting delights from stewards who met us on deck offering ice cream and tiny decorated cakes that melted in our mouths. We watched the horse races on the sports deck where little wooden horses were moved by long poles after a throw of some dice. The passengers wore jockeys' hats with green stripes and yellow bills.

A sign announced, "Three times around the deck and you have walked a mile." I circled the deck, hearing the sound of guns as passengers fired at skeets shot off the deck and flying high over the water. The sound of the gunfire frightened me.

Soon enough I walked the deck alone, because Peggy was seasick and getting all the attention. She said, "Only gumdrops make me feel better." I was disgusted by the number of gumdrops she was getting, but I couldn't get seasick.

When Peggy's stomach quieted down after a sufficient dose of gumdrops, we would eat with Mother and Daddy in the Grand Dining Room, entered by descending a sweeping staircase. On these occasions we were dressed alike; our hair, which had never been cut, was carefully curled around Mother's finger into long vertical curls. When so brushed and coiffed, people would call us the "Little English Girls."

Our young lives had two certainties: one that we were Marines, and secondly that, although we were only one-fourth English on our mother's side, someone would think we were British. When we arrived in the dining room, the waiters, resplendent in their white jackets and creased pants would greet us with, "Oh, it's the little English girls."

'We're not really English," we would explain. "We're Americans. We're Marines." But Mother had told us to be polite, and they were kind to us, so we accepted the title. We chose from a large menu that was printed daily and looked like a beautiful book. One night we sat at the Captain's Table: spotless white tablecloth, napkins folded intricately like birds about to take flight.

Breakfast and lunch were on the Sport Deck, and Peggy and I usually ate alone. We went to movies, watched puppet shows, and swam in the pool, feeling the ocean breezes getting warmer. Mother seemed happy. She and Daddy won the ship-wide bridge tournament, their trophy a fold-up alarm clock in a black leather case.

After five and one-half days heading west, Hawaii drew near. In another few hours, we would cling to the rail of the *Lurline* as we passed the first landfall, Koko Head, then Diamond Head, then Aloha Tower, crowning the final approach and dock of Honolulu. Outrigger canoes would race out to greet the ship, graceful tanned figures would dive into the harbor for coins, musicians with small stringed instruments and wearing brilliant floral shirts would play strange lilting music on the dock, and dancers dressed in halters and grass skirts would move their hips to the music. The air would be sweetened with scents foreign to us, ginger and pikaki. *Leis*, circlets of flowers, would bedeck our bodies.

But first, Mother surprised us by asking, "Do you girls want to select something from the gift shop?"

Down we went on the elevator to the shop full of treasures. I knew exactly what I wanted, because I had already been daydreaming in that shop: a sterling silver charm bracelet with a charm surfboard, some green enameled charm palm trees, some blue and green charm tropical fishes, and small letters, H A W A I I, linked in a diagonal line. The bracelet had spaces for more charms.

It rests in my jewelry box now, a memento of many things including the time in October of 1940 when we sailed westward, charmed by the music and the air and carried by a palace. Three new charms have been added: an identification circle with a San Francisco address; a red, white and blue "Remember Pearl Harbor" charm; and a tiny replica of a 32-caliber magazine loading machine gun.

Three

Everything about Hawaii was new and wonderful to our eyes. I felt cradled by the warm air that enveloped me. We'd arrived on the fifteenth of October. Daddy took command of the Marine Barracks on Ford Island on the sixteenth. And it was in a bungalow on the grounds of the Halekulani Hotel on Waikiki beach that Peggy had her tenth birthday, Janice Pritchard miraculously in attendance, on the eighteenth. Our new quarters were not ready, so it was in a bungalow by the beach in the shade of palm trees that our new lives began.

Everywhere we looked we could see the vivid colors and smell the scent of flowers: plumeria with its rich heavy aroma, single and doublefringed hibiscus in rich shades of gold, and orange, red, and purple bougainvillea arching high. And there were strange looking trees with even stranger names: monkey pod and banyan. The fruits from mango, coconut, and papaya trees spilled onto the ground, inviting a taste of the bounty. The grounds of the Halekulani were a jungle of trees that invited forays of discovery.

While our parents talked, Janice, Peggy and I explored, holding arms, walking down to the beach. It was empty, and we were temped to go into the water.

"Stop!" Janice commanded. "You have to wear shoes when you go in there. It's the coral growing under the

13

water. It's sharp and will cut your feet and cause an infection. You must wear sneakers in the water every place except in front of the Royal Hawaiian. They've cleared the beach in front of the hotel."

We examined the strange trees with wide trunks and many limbs; branches grew down from the limbs until they hit the ground then grew into it forming a new trunk. "These are Banyan trees," Janice informed us. "You can swing from the branches." She swung off into the air holding the ropelike limb in her hand. Soon we were swinging like monkeys, feeling wonderful and free.

What a strange new place Hawaii was, flowers free to be picked, fruit waiting to be harvested from the ground, trees that had branches you could swing on like Tarzan, people walking barefoot on the streets, and beaches whose waters you could enter only with shoes on! We had much to learn about our new home.

Our green Pontiac was soon disgorged from the cargo hold of the *Lurline*, and it was time to go on to Pearl Harbor. Honolulu seemed like a sleepy town as we drove through it. There were no traffic lights along Kalahaua Avenue, but the houses sported riots of color. Stretched along the fronts of the larger buildings were clotheslines crisscrossing, hung with all descriptions of clothing waving in the breeze like decorations.

We drove to Pearl Harbor on a two-lane country road that traversed fields of sugar cane. As we entered the main gate, the most commanding feature was the huge hammerhead crane, painted in large red and white squares, that dominated the scene and was used to raise and lower machinery from the dry-docks.

Daddy parked in front of a building and announced, "We have to stop here and get your dependent's passes made. Everyone going on Ford Island must have a pass.

There are two main rules you must learn about the base: always carry your identification, and never, never, take any pictures. You girls will have to put your Brownie cameras away."

Mothers and Peggy's ID pictures looked fine; mine more closely resembled a monkey. "Don't feel too bad, Joan," Mother said. "These passes are only good for a year. They'll expire December 31, 1941. You'll have another chance then."

It was now time for our first trip to Ford Island. What really surprised me was that we had to take a ferry to the island. The other islands we'd lived on -- North Island in San Diego and Yerba Buena Island in the middle of San Francisco Bay -- had been connected by a bridge to larger land. Not the case with Ford Island: the only way on or off was by ferry or boat. It you missed the hourly ferry, it was too bad. You waited. Our future lives were to be controlled by this faithful ferry.

There was an immense feeling of wonder as we left the slip on our first trip. Marines had saluted Daddy and welcomed him aboard; that was impressive. But it was the sight of the battleships, huge, glorious, strong, flags waving at their masts, that filled me with wonder. "That's Battleship Row," Daddy announced. "The ships are in," and as we rode by he named them: "*Arizona, Nevada, West Virginia, Tennessee, Oklahoma.*" Peggy and I waved as we sailed past; the men waved back. The ships and their men would become guardians of our lives.

Ford Island seen from the air today seems impossibly small: 450 acres, a mile and a quarter long and three-quarters of a mile wide, but in 1940 it would encompass our entire lives for fourteen months. The original Hawaiians called it "Mokuumeune," the Island of Strife. After being called "Rabbit Island," "Marin's Island," and

"Little Goats Island," it acquired its present name when Dr. Seth Porter Ford married the owner of the island in 1866.   From 1906 to 1917, the Oahu Sugar Company leased Ford Island and maintained it as a sugar cane plantation. The Army acquired it in 1917.   In 1923 the Pacific Air Detachment moved onto the island, joining the Army Air Corp which was using the west side of the island.

The Navy Department was subsequently given entire custody of the island, and the station grew in importance. President Roosevelt visited the island in 1934, and, when she was attempting her ill-fated flight around the world, Amelia Earhart crash-landed there on Luke Field, on March 20, 1936. The island was further developed as a result of the President's Emergency Proclamation of September 1939, when concrete hangars, offices, barracks, and other permanent building were constructed.

Daddy pointed out the hangars, dispensary, red and white striped air tower, and Luke Field as we headed for the southeastern portion of the island. In contrast to all the cement and asphalt of the naval installations, this end of the island was ethereally quiet. Langley Road paralleled the island's shore, leading us to our new quarters, Quarters T.

Daddy stopped the car in front of a gentle green house facing the harbor. I looked at the quarters, my mind taking pictures: click, click, click. There was a front lawn, a narrow street, another stretch of lawn, a small expanse of water, and then the ships, Battleship Row. The ships paraded in majesty just five hundred feet from Quarters T.

The beauty of the moment was imprinted on my mind. The air was filled with sounds from the ships, and then, suddenly, the bells began to toll. I counted one, two, three, all the way up to eight. Perplexed, I looked at Daddy.

"Eight bells," he explained. "That means it's twelve o'clock. We will be able to tell time by the ships. We won't need a clock here on Ford Island."

"We can't go in yet. They're still getting it ready for us," Mother said, "but you can see the quarters from the road. What we're here for today is to enroll you in school."

And that is how we were enrolled in what I considered to be the perfect place.

Kenneth Whiting School, we were to learn, was named for Captain Kenneth Whiting, a pioneer Navy pilot who'd been taught to fly by Orville Wright. One of Whiting's earliest accomplishments was to demonstrate how one could exit a torpedo tube of a submarine and survive. He was a hero, and the school followed in his traditions. Mrs. Uhler, a cousin of Captain Whiting, was the principal, and Miss Greeny McVey was to be my teacher. Knowing that her students would be from all over the United States, Mrs. Uhler had written to different schools on what was soon to become a familiar term to us, "the Mainland," to model a curriculum that would keep her students happy.

The school itself was about three hundred yards from Quarters T. It was a long low building surrounded by grassy playgrounds. Since our quarters weren't ready yet, we would have to travel to and from school from Honolulu. Mrs. Uhler instructed Mother, "Be sure to get *lauhala* mats for the girls, because every day we have a rest period on the *lanai*."

The ferry took us back across the harbor, and we headed back to Honolulu. I had a strange feeling that Ford Island was a place of enormous power and strength, but also something that had to be protected.

We had never had to put away our cameras before, or to have identification passes, either. We listened quietly; we were Marines taking orders.

"Watch your head, Miss," the sailor cautioned as he took my hand, the one that wasn't holding my new rolled up *lauhala* mat, and helped me into the launch. It was our first day of school, and we were on the last leg of our journey to Ford Island. First we'd taken the Oahu Railway to the terminal at the end of the line. Then a Navy bus had taken us to the small launch ramp by the ferry. Pearl City children, from the far side of the harbor, had joined us on the launch. And, finally, a Navy launch scooted us across the harbor, past the ships, and deposited us at a landing by the ferry. Another bus picked us up and took us to school.

"This is the *lanai*," Mrs. Uhler said in greeting. "I see you have your *lauhala* mats. At 11:00 every student rolls them out and rests on the *lanai*. We use Hawaiian words here. *Lanai* means porch. *Opu* is your stomach, and you're a *wahini*, a girl."

The *lanai* with its screen windows stretched across the front of the school. The classrooms opened onto it. The classrooms went by grades: the fifth and sixth grades were next to Enterprise Road, and the library was at the other end by the water. School started at eight o'clock, there was a snack break at ten, the no-talking rest at eleven, and then school was over at one o'clock, before it got too hot.

I inspected the library carefully; it was full of interesting books. I rejoiced. They had already started fractions; this school was not behind. We rolled out our new mats, made of tightly woven reeds. I lay dreaming, watching the shadows of the trees as they swayed in the balmy breeze outside the building. I was at peace.

At one o'clock we started our launch-bus-streetcar return to the hotel, stopping at the terminal for ice cream cones. These were special cones because way down deep in the cone, after all the ice cream had been eaten, was a piece of white paper that when unfolded invariably said, "free cone." Another wonder.

And then it was November and we moved.

Major Adolph Zuber, U.S.M.C.
Quarters T

Daddy's official nameplate hung from the standard in front of our new home. We were officially in residence, and I loved Quarters T. It was filled with sunshine.

And it had four doors out. I always counted the doors out. This was the thirteenth place we'd lived in, and all the rest had only had one or two doors leading out. It was wonderful to have so many ways to enter and exit, to be able to choose what experience you wished.

The front door opened into a foyer. To the left was the living room with its huge lava stone fireplace. This room was formal with the rugs, chow bench, camphor chest, nested tables, and wall hangings that Daddy had brought home from China. It was not a place for playing. Opening from it to the left was the *lanai*, and a glass door that opened out to a row of tall hibiscus bushes. Two walls of screened glass windows welcomed the sun that flooded the room with warmth. Looking through the windows, I could see the water tower, airfield and hangars. The *lanai*, where Mother had placed the rattan furniture, was my favorite room. I loved to sit on the flowered chaise lounge chair and read. The only battle I would ever encounter here before

December seventh was between the ever-present ants and a caterpillar that had lost its way. The kitchen was behind the *lanai*, with a door leading to the laundry room -- with another door to the side yard -- and finally a maid's room and bath.

Straight across from the front entry was the entrance to the dining room with its wall of windows. Another door led out to the rear garden, where a host of papaya trees dropped their fruit on the grass. Daddy loved to open this door and, with his arms spread out and feet firmly in place, entice us to try to get through. "Aha, I've got you now!" he would exclaim. We would defeat him by going through his legs.

In addition to the dining room's wall of windows and glass, there was a metal button underneath the table on the floor that, when depressed, rang a bell in the kitchen. "That's for the maid," Mother explained. Peggy and I practiced pushing the button, pretending that someone would open the swinging door from the kitchen and ask us, "What do you wish?"

So the left hand side of the quarters was a circular route that connected the living room, *lanai*, kitchen, dining room, and front entry. But that was only the left hand side of Quarters T. A hall led from the right of the entry to two bedrooms that faced Battleship Row. Mother claimed the first one by depositing her sewing machine, typewriter, and a strange metal dressmaking form that looked like a headless lady in the corners of the room.

"Your father's snoring always keeps me awake, and he's so big. He might roll over and crush me. The master bedroom will be his," Mother explained. I knew that Daddy had a fearsome snore, but I liked the sound. When Mother and Daddy went out, I would wake up in the middle of the night and, hearing his snore, know that we were again safe and all together. There was a small bathroom with a shower off his room. We called it his "library" because he went in there regularly every morning and read the paper, *Time* or *Life*.

Peggy and I shared a third bedroom. Ours faced the rear yard opposite from the front bedrooms. We had a fifth way out, a low window opening to the rear yard. Last of all, there was our bathroom with an ample tub for blowing bubbles.

To the rear of the quarters was a covered carport where we kept our bikes and the 1939 green Pontiac. Daddy kept his Shopsmith and woodworking materials in a small room attached to the carport. He'd already begun working on a new project: a tabletop game in which two players moved wooden dowels with hanging paddles to strike or block balls.

But the most beautiful of all sights was when we looked out the front windows in the living room, the front bedrooms, or the *lanai,* or when we walked out the front door: the ships. We listened to the ships' bells, the boatswains' whistles, even the music to which the men did their early calisthenics. Each morning our feet, too, kept time to Souza's "El Capitan" or "Hands Across the Sea," as we marched to school waving to our neighbors on the ships.

We'd only been on the island a week when I was told that I was going to die, a victim of an algarroba tree. It was late afternoon when I went exploring, alone, to the school playground and the cluster of bungalows that edged it. In school we had met the children who lived there in Quarters 28 through 32. "Do you want to go swinging?" they questioned, leading me over to a tree with a rope swing that swung out over the harbor towards the *U.S.S. Oklahoma*.

"Ouch!" I exclaimed as I swung to and fro. Sharp needles had pierced my arm, and it was bleeding.

"Get off carefully," the children yelled. "That is an algarroba tree. If you have been stung by its needles, you will die."

I began to cry: I was going to die on the playground of Kenneth Whiting School. I curled up in a ball; the only dead person I'd ever seen was Grandfather Zuber lying in state in his coffin in the parlor of his New Jersey, home. Even the kiss I had finally gotten the courage to give him had not resurrected him.

Shocked by my quick reaction to their fatal diagnosis, the children chorused, "It's just a joke! We were only teasing you." But I could not believe them. They brought hibiscus flowers, dropping them into my lap, tucking them into my hair. "Look, you are a princess." I didn't believe them. I could feel the poison entering my body. The only way I could get home to Daddy and have him help me die was to agree with them, smile, and run back to Quarters T.

"Joan, you're all right. They were playing a prank on you, the new kid on the island," Daddy laughed as he looked at my wounds. But I didn't feel all right for awhile, and for the rest of the time I lived in Hawaii I gave any algarroba tree a wide berth.

Peggy and I soon became part of the rhythm of that part of the island now called "Nob Hill." which encompassed Quarters A through T. The harbor, or "drink" as we sometimes called it, formed a natural boundary. We were warned by our friends not to climb on the big wide pipes that encircled our end of the island, or to play on the narrow shoreline. "Quicksand, it's *kapu*, forbidden," instructed our new friend, Ann Dale O'Brien. Walking on Luke Field two hundred yards across Saratoga Boulevard was expressly forbidden. Families lived in three different places: the five Noncommissioned Officers' Quarters by Kenneth Whiting School, twenty officers' quarters on "Nob Hill," and fifteen additional quarters across Luke Field on Yorktown Boulevard. The paths around the quarters, with their banyan trees and gardens, became our giant communal playground.

Right behind Quarters T was the Officers' Swimming Pool and a small, less formal Officers' Club that boasted snacks and slot machines. As soon as school was out, lunches eaten and digested, everyone met at the pool. Peggy and I felt very grown up, putting nickels in the slot machines, winning sometimes, cheering as the nickels poured out. It wasn't a smart idea showing Daddy our pile of nickels. "I don't think you girls should be playing the slots," he replied. Sure enough, a new rule was posted: "No children may play the slot machines." But we could still get Cokes and swim all afternoon.

The pool boasted a low and a high diving board, with umbrella tables, chairs, and chaise lounges on the concrete apron surrounding it. Ford Island children were water nymphs, but the best swimmers were the O'Brien family; Ann Dale and her five-year old brother were the stars. Ann went off the high diving board with regularity, but her brother often did a belly flop with a smack that made concentric waves.

The only days we were not supposed to go swimming were when they were cleaning the pool. Mother made the announcement, "You cannot go swimming today. They are changing the pool's water." And then she seemed to disappear. We weren't sure where she'd gone, but we knew where we were going: swimming. In our sun suits we took the fifth exit out of the quarters, our bedroom window. I played around in the low water, but Peggy jumped in unaware that the pool wasn't full enough to cushion her jump. "My heels hurt," she said softly. We went home, checked to see where Mother was, climbed back through the window, and changed into dry clothes. Peggy was very quiet. "If I tell Mother about my heels, she'll know we disobeyed." I heard her moving about in her bed, trying to get comfortable. She suffered in silence.

Injuries aside, we swam every day, turned brown with the sun, and toughened our feet by rubbing them on the asphalt streets. Children did not wear shoes on Ford Island; we wore "go aheads," so named because, in these mat sandals with thongs to thread your toes through, you could only go ahead. If you backed up, the sandals came off. We were becoming *kama'ainas*, old timers on Ford Island. Rain was not rain to us now; it was "liquid sunshine," and we reveled in its touch.

Mother was quieter in Hawaii. She didn't lead the Girl Scouts as she had in Quantico.

Nor did she teach Sunday School. We'd always attended church regularly. Military Chaplains were of many different denominations, but with men who might, as the Navy Hymn says, "perish on the sea," and with their dependents so far from home, church services gave unity to our lives. My favorite hymn was "The Church by the Side of the Road" from my *New Hymnal for Christian Youth*. Its final line, "Wherever you roam, it is calling you home," gave a sense of permanence to my young life.

But Mother's gaiety was gone. Ferdinand, the ceramic bull that graced the credenza in our new dining room, reminded me of better times. When Munroe Leaf, the author of *The Story of Ferdinand the Bull*, had come to San Francisco in 1939, she'd met him, received an

24

autographed book, bought the ceramic bull, and then made an ingenious cork tree for him to sit under.

"Dolph, I don't like the news. England is getting bombed every day. I feel war coming closer and closer." Mother was talking to Daddy late at night.

He tried to reassure her. "Alice, try not to worry. We are safe here."

"Are we?" she replied. "I don't think so. I sense danger." I didn't understand what she meant. It seemed so safe here.

Thanksgiving and Christmas of 1940 came, and we celebrated with our family tradition, the making of the stuffing. Peggy and I would crumb the bread while Mother chopped the onions and celery. We'd sauté these in butter, then add the crumbs and hot water. "Taste it, girls. Is it good?" Mother would ask, giving us two long wooden handled spoons for the tasting. The tasting ceremony would take a long time. Dashes of poultry seasoning and pats of butter would be added until the announcement came, "It's just right." Peggy graduated that Christmas, becoming the onion chopper; I continued being the shredder and peeler.

We were having more success with our cake-baking experiments. Our earlier efforts, usually when Mother and Daddy were out, sometimes ended up on the kitchen floor. In consequence, our icing techniques to disguise the fractured layers had improved. We would cream the butter, add the powdered sugar, mix in a few drops of food coloring, slaver the icing on and present our offering for dessert.

But cakes and stuffing aside, our Christmas of 1940 was different. When Mother asked me what I wanted I immediately replied, "A Story Book Doll, 'Thursday's Child Has Far to Go'." I had been born on a Thursday and really wanted that doll. It was there for me under the tree, but when Janice called and invited us into Honolulu on Christmas afternoon, I didn't have a present for her.

"Well, Joan, give her one of your own. Give her the one you like the most, and I'll replace it."

So I wrapped up Thursday's Child and gave it to Janice. As the weeks passed after Christmas and no doll appeared, I realized that Mother had forgotten her promise. It was not like her to forget something so completely. She was becoming increasingly quiet. She was sick more often, and, although already very thin, she began to lose more weight.

And then, surprisingly, she said we could have kittens. Cats overran the island, progeny of an orange king cat, the island mascot, named Butterball. It seemed that everyone had a cat. We'd been imploring Mother to let us have kittens, and she finally acquiesced. Snowball, called Snowy, an all white kitten, was Peggy's. Mine was a tiger I named Rainbow, "Rainy" for short. Rainy was an apt name, because she subsequently rained all over the quarters. "Joan," my mother would call, "Rainy's gone behind the water heater in the laundry room again." That was my command to take care of Rainy's messes. In addition to her indiscretion, Rainy never cleaned herself. It was up to Snowy, through numerous lickings, to cleanse Rainy.

One day I decided to give Snowy a hand, using the bottle of "Bug-Off" in the bathroom. The application didn't bother Rainy, but Snowy almost died. She hid beneath Peggy's bed beside a lake of green excrement for days. Mother was her doctor, I her nurse. She finally recovered, only to meet another fate.

Late one night I heard Mother discussing with one of Daddy's Marines cats and the relative depths of water off Ford Island. The Marine had gunny sacks in his hands. Both cats disappeared that night. Rainy returned after a few days, only to disappear again. I did not discuss the disappearance with Peggy; I only wished that Mother had given us a choice. I'd have chosen Snowy.

Butterball, the grand sire, met a similar fate in 1942, but as a victim both of war and his astonishing virility. Months after we were evacuated, Daddy wrote that the Commanding Officer of the Naval Air Station had arrived in his office one morning only to discover a cat and her newly borne litter of five kittens reposing in his cherished upholstered chair. All cats were thenceforth banished from the island. Butterball, the island mascot, was adopted and was being flown to the mainland by his new owner. However, the plane crashed into San Francisco Bay, and the pilot and all passengers were lost.

Sometimes, tiring of swimming, Peggy and I would just wander off quietly to play in the sandbox on the playground of Kenneth Whiting School. We filled buckets of water from the nearby spigot and added the sand to achieve just the right consistency. "These are skyscrapers," explained Peggy as she molded tall forms. I would dig the tunnels and build bridges. Planes droned like bees at Luke Field one hundred yards away, their sounds mixed in with the toot of the ferry and the bells of the ships. Shadows would lengthen as we worked: the masts of the ships etched the playground, acting as sundials, marking the passage of time.

We were recreating the land of the future, Futurama, that we had seen four thousand miles away at the 1940 World's Fair in New York City a year ago with all the bridges, subways, tunnels, skyscrapers, and cars. Mrs. Uhler, ever diligent even after school hours, did not like our new world. She called Mother, "Peggy and Joan are wetting the sand. They're too old." We were "too old" at nine and ten. The fragile Futurama collapsed and turned back into grains of sand.

The Old BOQ (Bachelor Officers' Quarters) was called "old" because it was one of the oldest buildings on the island and was being replaced by the concrete New BOQ across the island. The Old BOQ stood next to Quarters T and invited exploration. It was a big two-story brown shingle building with a banyan tree gracing its front. We'd been warned to respect the privacy of the men, but we walked around the building, trying to appear casual. The living quarters were in front, the kitchen and delivery area in the rear facing Lexington Boulevard. Brown latticework covered the open basement, but Peggy and I discovered an opening on the side facing our quarters.

We entered, examining the concrete pillars that supported the building. "Look at that!" I exclaimed, pointing. There, painted on the pillar, was a huge black swastika, a frightening thing to see on this peaceful island. Peggy and I knew what the swastika meant: Daddy had bought a short wave radio to keep abreast of the news oversees. I'd given my globe to the class at school so we could watch the changing boundaries. And at night we could hear Mother and Daddy talking. "Danger," "the Japanese," "scrap iron," "oil," and "military buildup." We backed out quickly, vowing not to tell Daddy, and we never went under the Old BOQ again.

Four

1941

"Girls, you'll have to entertain yourselves more of the time. I'm going into Honolulu for classes," Mother announced one morning in February of 1941. By this time, such a challenge was not a problem. We'd lived on Ford Island for four months, and Peggy and I had made friends all over the island. There were Tommy and Jimmy Shoemaker, the Captain's sons; Ann Dale O'Brien; Margaret Grant; Drule; and Eleanor Bellinger, the Admiral's daughter. We played, swam, and went to movies together. But our favorite pastime was to meet and hide in Eleanor Bellinger's dungeon.

In 1917, two turret gun emplacements had been built, protected with concrete, and connected to storage and ammunition rooms, facing Aiea and McGrew Point. Germans were the danger even in 1917, and it was felt that if German warships entered Pearl Harbor and circled Ford Island towards Aiea, the guns would be there to stop them. If they missed the enemy warships, the shells would fall harmlessly in the sugar cane fields beyond. By 1936, the danger was felt to have passed and the Admiral's Quarters, to be known as Quarters K, was constructed using the guns' installation site as the quarter's foundation. The spot had an unparalleled view.

What fun we had in the dungeon! Our imaginations scampered along with us between the sinister concrete walls forming the long halls between cannon emplacements, and through barred doors leading to what we considered cells. The large opening of the gun emplacement on the right side of the dungeon had been walled, creating a dark concrete room, but the aperture on the left side was still open, affording us a wide view of the harbor. "Let's play Sardines," the call would go out, and half a dozen of us would scurry about in our little cotton playsuits to find the one hiding and squeeze in with her or him. The last one to find us was the new "it."

Usually the wide dungeon hall was filled with the echoes of our voices, footsteps, and laughter, but when we played Sardines we were quiet, walking softly on our bare feet, hoping that the dark barred rooms were empty of ghosts. It was a place of noisy play and quiet suspense.

Several weeks after Mother had made her announcement, she explained. "I'm taking First Aid classes. I want to be ready. All the Marine wives in Pearl Harbor are learning First Aid." Her face was not smiling as she repeated, "We want to be ready."

She didn't tell us exactly what it was she wanted to be ready for, but we soon tired of her practicing her new skills on us. Over and over, she'd put splints on our arms and legs and check our eyes with her flashlight. As the weeks passed, we tried not to be home when we saw the ferry bringing her Pontiac back to Ford Island; we feared whatever new skill she was going to want to practice on us.

Our father also grew impatient with her odd new avocation. "Alice, come here," Daddy called one morning after his stint in his "library" reading the newspaper. He got out a pair of scissors, cut out a poem, and pinned it to the kitchen wall. "Here's something for you to read."

Peggy and I clustered next to her as she read it aloud. "Lady, if you see me lying/ on the ground and maybe dying/ pass me by and leave me be/ please don't practice your First Aid on me."

Mother threw back her head and laughed. It felt so good to hear her laugh. She knew we were her victims. " I'll keep that poem with me always." But then her thin face grew serious. "Dolph, when it comes, I want to be ready. I want to be able to help."

Mother wasn't laughing when she arrived home from her final class on March 11, 1941, holding her card from The American National Red Cross certifying that she'd completed the Standard Course of Instruction in First Aid to the Injured at Honolulu, Territory of Hawaii. One of the ladies, practicing resuscitation skills on Mother, had pushed too hard that day and cracked two of her ribs. Her chest trussed up in bandages, Mother nevertheless drove us girls into Honolulu for a celebratory treat. I don't know what else we did that day, but I do know what Mother got: Tropical Fever.

We were thirsty and stopped for cool drinks. Bireley's Grape was my favorite, Peggy's also. We liked it straight from the bottle using a straw, the way Aunt Peggy had shown us how to drink when she'd visited us on Yerba Buena. But Mother was uneasy: "Girls, you shouldn't drink straight out of bottles, even with a straw. It's unladylike. Pour it into a glass." We pressed a bit and she acquiesced: "Well, you can this time, but I'm going to have a glass of ice water. I'll drink mine out of the glass, the proper way." By that evening, Mother was running a temperature and vomiting. The doctor diagnosed that she had picked up the Tropical Fever bacteria from her improperly washed glass. She was hospitalized for about a week.

Even though we'd had "help" at home on Ford Island earlier, by the time of Mother's hospitalization we girls were on our own. In the four and one-half months we'd lived there, the maid's room had had two occupants. The first was Anna, wife of a sailor who was off on sea duty. Anna made the best pork pie; we looked forward to Thursdays when she took the afternoon off and left one steaming on the kitchen counter. She was short and plump with white hair curling around her face. For the first few weeks of her regime, I'd thought she was a spy, because on the dresser in her room she had a picture of her husband standing in front of the Ford Island hangars. But I decided not to report her to Daddy, because she didn't look dangerous. Then Anna's husband came home from sea duty, she left, and another, younger woman moved into the maid's room.

Donna's tenure was even shorter-lived. She was young, had bright red hair, and talked with Daddy's men. Although Mother had left strict instructions about our bedtime, Donna let us stay up late one night playing board games alone in our room.

When the lights of the approaching Pontiac lit up our bedroom announcing that my parents were back, Donna raced into the room, turned off the lights, and told us to get into bed.

Well, she didn't fool Mother. After firing Donna, Mother came into our room, roused us from our beds, and gave us a spanking for being part of the deception.

"That's not fair," we chorused.

"You didn't follow orders," Mother replied. "I fired Donna." I already knew that being fired was not actually being set ablaze, but the consequences were just

32

as complete. Donna was gone the next morning, having lasted only a week. "She was playing around," Mother announced.

I didn't think she meant Monopoly. Peggy and I wondered what game she had played.

With Mother in the hospital and on the "sick list," Peggy and I were left further to our own devices. We became maids doing chores around the house, carefully introducing the clothes into the old wringer washing machine. Mother had told us horror stories about the wringer and what had happened to little girls who didn't let go when the sturdy rubber rollers ate up the clothes, squeezing the water out. We hung the clothes on the clothesline in the back of the quarters, reaching tall to push the wooden clothespins over the fabric and the cord.

While she was recovering, Daddy also helped out. He was now the one who took us places -- swimming, up across the Pali, out to Waimea Beach with its huge waves, and into Honolulu to visit Colonel and Mrs. Davidson, our Marine Corp friends.

Peggy had begun keeping a diary in a composition book from school. How innocently the days passed as Peggy recorded the movies we saw, the small argument she had with our friend Eleanor, and her feeling of glee when Eleanor fell off her bike as we were being chauffeured in Daddy's station wagon. Peggy wrote about her infected foot and that its treatment necessitated a doctor's visit and a two-hour wait at the Naval Dispensary.

And then in a few simple lines she recorded on March 23, 1941: "Sunday. Went swimming at Mag Davidson's. Had Good dinner. Got a cut from coral!! Went to sleep two times, twenty minutes. Got caught on blackout, had to stay on dock until boat came." How insidiously it all began, the black outs and joint air raid drills that were held weekly on Ford Island beginning in the spring of 1941. We children began preparing for war, not knowing what war was.

"Why are we having blackouts and drills here, Daddy?" I asked. We knew all about the air raids in Europe.

"We have to be prepared in case of an attack. We want to be sure that everybody knows what to do and where to go," he answered.

"In a black-out, a wailing siren sounds and everyone has to turn off all their lights." My father's face kept smiling, but his words were grave. "In the air-raid drills, you must immediately leave for the shelter. Ours is the dungeon under Admiral Bellinger's quarters." At home, when a siren would sound our family would practice turning the lights off and hovering in the dark, trying to imagine what would happen if real planes were flying over. We'd look out our windows. Our neighbors' lights would all be out, and so were all the lights on all the ships.

During the air-raid drills, we practiced the run to the dungeon: hear the siren, dash out the back door, make a sharp left turn then a sharp right hand turn onto Lexington behind the Old BOQ, veer left, run down to the *cul de sac* in front of Bay's home, and go down the sloping drive on the left to the entrance of the dungeon. Run, run. Take roll. Wait for the "all clear." We talked as we retraced our steps home, our children's voices belying the gravity of the contents of our words.

Even after Mother was released from the hospital, she couldn't get around very well for several weeks. Daddy's drivers, who drove his official white station wagon, pitched in and helped us out. Every day the Naval Air Station put out "Daily Notices." The page, with a masthead of wings and a shield with Naval Air Station at the top, listed what the weather would be like, the movies that were being shown, the Daily Routine, and Special Notices. In the grand old theater with its massive curtain, trellised sides, and palm fronds bordering the stage, movies started at 1600 hours, which meant four o'clock. Peggy and I would choose the movie and then ask for Daddy's drivers.

It was so different on Ford Island from anywhere else we'd ever lived. Everyone was so much friendlier; we didn't ever worry about strangers.

When we'd lived on the U.S. Naval Air Station North Island in San Diego, our parents had told us never to accept a ride from anyone. We had been late getting out of a movie there, and, missing the last bus, decided to walk home. As we'd approached the airfield, we'd been ordered off by a scary voice. We'd continued on, skirting the airfield. Two of Daddy's men had recognized us and offered us a ride home. "We're not allowed to talk to strangers," we'd replied to their request. That left the men in a bind: what would Major Zuber think if we got hurt on the way home? Finally they resolved the dilemma by calling Mother.

On Ford Island, by contrast, we were safe and we really liked Daddy's drivers. Sometimes they would drive us to the movie theater or the Officers' Club for an early dinner. I was not sure which I liked better, the trip in the station wagon to the movies or the dinner beforehand. We could order anything we wanted, but I was most interested in the dessert: chocolate sundaes served in silver bowls. Then I refined my choice to chocolate sundae without the ice cream. I would spoon up the thick chocolate syrup, scraping for the last drop.

Daddy really liked his men; he would counsel them, laugh with them. Sometimes he'd get letters from their parents asking him to "keep your eye out for them." One of them was a boxer whose career Peggy and I followed. "How was your fight? Did you win?"

"I lost," Clint said sadly. "But there's a next time." We prayed he would win.

Mother was recovering and getting stronger, but I began feeling left out. She and Peggy started sharing a secret. I knew it was a secret. They didn't whisper, but I would walk into a room when they were talking and they would look at me and change the subject of their conversation.

Peggy was now almost eleven, and I was nine and a half. Up until this time, we had always been dressed alike and never compared. Mother had a thing about comparisons. She had even written an article about comparisons and sent it into a magazine stating, "It is wrong to talk about how handsome or beautiful brother or sister is and how you wish the child's hair or feet or any manner of physical appearance were like theirs." So there were no comparisons in our house, but that didn't stop me from making comparisons about myself.

I had worn glasses since the age of seven, diagnosed with myopia and a lazy eye. The eye doctor had prescribed a black patch to be worn over my right eye. Mother went to school and discussed this with my second grade teacher. "You could tell the class that Joan is a pirate." Well, that did not go over with me. Each day as I walked to school I dropped the patch into the weeds that grew beside the sidewalk. After five patches disappeared, Mother gave up.

I got rid of the patches but not the glasses, and, unfortunately, they made me different. Often Kenneth Whiting School's Miss McVey did not understand. One day after a volleyball game, I put my hand to my glasses and discovered the right lens was missing. Miss McVey, not realizing why I was so worried, initially would not excuse me to look for it. On my hands and knees, I combed the grass on the volleyball court, finally found the lens, pushed it back into the frame and returned happily to class.

Mother may have stopped other people's comparisons, but not my own. I was sure that Peggy was prettier than I was, and "Lei Day" was my proof. In Hawaii the first of May is Lei Day, a special holiday celebrated with flowers, *leis*, a Maypole and a May Queen. That was the secret Mother and Peggy had been sharing. Peggy's teacher, Mrs. Baread, told all the fourth and fifth graders at school that Peggy was going to be Queen of the May, a very important role. Mrs. Baread didn't say it, but I felt certain that only the prettiest girl was selected. Now we were compared at school. Peggy was pretty, I wore glasses. I was different.

Bay Bellinger was to be Mistress of Ceremonies; her mother took her into Honolulu to buy a long dress, but Mother, recovering and still too thin, was determined to sew Peggy's. She and Peggy planned a confection of organdy and lace. I was to be a flower; all the girls my age were to wear different colors of crepe paper dresses. Peggy was going to be beautiful

Mother bought yards and yards of white organdy and lace at the yardage store in Honolulu. She then had a seamstress divide the organdy into two-inch wide strips by making a lock stitch the lengths of material. She separated the strips with scissors at home, cutting carefully between the lock stitches. Then she began combining them back together and inserting the lace. Organdy, lace, organdy, lace.

"Alice, I think you're making this dress too complicated," Daddy said. "You know how long it takes you to sew. It's only two weeks until May Day."

37

"I'll have it ready. It'll be fit for a queen."

I didn't want to think about the crepe paper dress; somebody else was making those.

Everyday we practiced the program at school. The crepe paper flowers sang songs from the stage. Yellow costumes and caplets were worn by the younger girls; the younger boys wore paper pods and jumped out like seeds. Tommy and Jimmy were to be dressed in white pants and white shirts along with the other older boys, and were to be part of Peggy's formal procession. We flowers practiced weaving the Maypole with strands of different colored ribbons. We circled in and out, in and out, until we were perfect.

May First came, and while Peggy's dress was ready, it was transparent and Mother had yet to make a slip. The program was going to start in one-half hour and there was still no slip.

Daddy came home, looked at the slip material, took a pair of scissors, cut it into pieces, and sat down at Mother's sewing machine. I will never forget the picture of my football-playing father in full military uniform sitting on the small wooden chair, sewing the slip. Within minutes it was ready, and Peggy was dressed: a dream in white.

I rustled in my coral-colored paper dress.

We were late to the ceremony. All the other parents and friends sat on folding chairs on the lawn; Mother and Daddy had to stand in back. "I'm sorry I'm late," Peggy said breathlessly as she placed the double hibiscus *lei* around her neck and crown on her head.

"I'm sorry too," stern Mrs. Ulner replied.

The piano began to play, and the celebration began. Peggy made her grand march followed by her escorts in white, and Bay announced the program. We sang, the seedlings popped out of their pods, and the capletted flowers danced. We stood and smiled in the gentle air of the tropical afternoon.

The ships were out of port, so there was no tolling of bells. The planes were not landing on Luke Field that day. The air was filled with our voices. Inside I was almost sick from the envy. Tears gathered right behind my eyeglassed eyes. I hoped desperately for next year.

And then Peggy was mad at me. Not speaking to me, she looked at me with that expression she always had that said, "How could you have done it?"

I knew that I'd caused it. Tommy Shoemaker had asked Peggy to let him kiss her and she'd said, "No!" He'd asked the other girls too, and they had echoed Peggy's answer.

But when he asked me, I thought, "Why not?"

Tommy and I planned it very carefully at the pool one afternoon. We were taking a break from swimming, and Peggy was in the clubhouse. "We'll do it tonight," I suggested.

"But how?" Tommy asked.

"We'll meet at nine o'clock tonight in the storeroom by the garage where Daddy keeps his Shopsmith. The door is unlocked. You be hiding there. I'll tell Peggy we're meeting there, but not why."

"But how?" Tommy asked.

I had given it a great deal of thought and replied, "I'll tell Peggy to kiss me, and then you come in between and kiss me instead."

I was a little nervous explaining to Peggy that we were going to go out to the storeroom, and I didn't wear anything special because it was going to be dark and Peggy would wonder why I was getting dressed up to go the storeroom. I sneaked into Mother's room and found her perfume, "Derkiss," the kind that she liked with the violets on the label. I dabbed a little of it carefully behind my ears and on my wrists. Then Peggy and I walked quietly out the dining room door, through the back yard, and to the storeroom.

We opened the storeroom door, entered, and carefully closed it. She reached for the string to turn on the overhead light. It wouldn't come on; earlier, I had loosened the bulb. The smell of sawdust from Daddy's latest project filled my nose and I sneezed.

But everything went as planned. I asked Peggy for a kiss, Tommy's head appeared in between us, and I got my kiss.

It wasn't great. I turned and ran quickly out the door and over the path to the house, leaving Tommy and Peggy behind. I dashed into the bathroom and scoured my face thoroughly with a rough face cloth. Peggy followed me, fuming.

"How could you do it?" she yelled. "I really like him! How could you do it?"

So I was really in the doghouse. Peggy wasn't speaking to me, and I wasn't speaking to Tommy. But those were the days of innocence. It had been nice in the storeroom squeezed between the wall and Daddy's Shopsmith. It was safe and we were young.

Five

Some of the darknesses of the adult world began to impact us. The first was Yuki, who entered our lives at the beginning of June. She was Japanese-American. Mother interviewed her for the maid's position. Peggy and I were thrilled with the idea that we might be released from chore duty, but more than that we fell in love with Yuki. She was exotic with long almost black hair that trailed down her back. Stocky, probably in her late thirties, she had a laugh that charmed us. Besides, during the initial interview she asked us what we would like as a present.

"*Nancy Drew books,*" we replied. I had already read many of the library books at Kenneth Whiting School, and *Nancy Drew* books, with all thier mysteries, were currency on the island, traded among our friends. We started dreaming about all the books Yuki would give us. When Yuki moved into her room, she gave us our present, A big foot long toy tank, the kind that when wound up with a key would move and roll over. It was unwrapped, and we wondered why she'd picked this gift.

Any disappointment we had ended when we saw her room; a big three-foot loom with the beginnings of a design on its threads. "I'll show you how to weave," Yuki announced. "This is how you place the yarn." Peggy and I were entranced; we listened to her

41

directions carefully. Then, when she was helping Mother, we got on our bikes and raced to tell all the girls that we would soon be weaving new clothes.

Two nights later I heard Yuki crying and talking to Mother in the living room. I couldn't hear what they were saying, so I asked Mother in the morning.

She looked at me quietly and said, "Joan, everyone on the island has to be investigated to see if they have a criminal record. If a person has a criminal record, they cannot work here."

"What is a record? What did Yuki do?"

"Yuki is a kleptomaniac. A kleptomaniac is someone who sees something, likes it, and takes it without paying."

Is that how she got the tank? I wondered. Is that why it came unwrapped?

How did she hide the tank when she took it out of the store?

Mother interrupted my thinking, saying, "I told Yuki that I'd vouch for her; that I would tell them that she's not a real thief, and that she's trying to stop."

I was relieved. Yuki would not have to go and we would learn how to weave. But then Yuki went into Honolulu on her first weekend off and didn't return. Mother explained her absence to us, "You have to understand. I really liked Yuki, but when she went into Honolulu she saw two fifty-dollar bills, thought they were pretty, and took them. She's in jail."

Yuki's clothes and her loom were packed and removed by her family. I read the newspaper every day trying to find out what had happened to her. A small notice finally appeared in the paper: she'd been sentenced and sent to prison. We missed her.

The pit opened in my stomach by Yuki was followed by an afternoon movie. "I wish I'd never seen it," Peggy said as we were driven home from the movies in Daddy's white station wagon.

"It really scared me," Anne Dale replied. "I didn't like the kidnapper and how he tried to steal the Mask of Kahn."

"And after he attacks the man and women, he takes off his mask and turns out to be a crazed astronomer. Who thought that up? It was scary," I added. "The Face Behind the Mask" was part of the double bill at the base theater. The first movie was good, but the mask was just too evil. We left, scared clear through.

But summer was here. We wore our playsuits and were tanned down to the soles of our feet. We formed a club, "The Firecrackers," based on the *Adventure Girls* books that we read along with *Nancy Drew*. Ann O'Brien was the President. She was very thin and had short dark hair and an oval face.

Dark-haired Drule, who was smaller than the rest of us, compact, freckled, and energetic, was Writer.

Margaret Grant, the Vice President, was taller and heavier and had red hair framing a round face.

I was Treasurer, and Peggy was Secretary. Peggy and I had the same dark brown, never-been-cut curly hair that hung down our backs. Peggy was older and taller. I had glasses; she didn't.

We picked aliases that Peggy duly recorded in her diary. Ann became "Gale," Peggy, "Valerie," and I picked "Phyllis," all character names from the *Adventure Girls* books.

We began to call Eleanor by a new name, "Bay." Her hair was blond and wavy, ending just above her shoulders, and she was rounded and graceful. We would play over at Bay's quarters above the dungeon. Her older sister Patricia had the most wonderful dollhouse on the left wall of her room. It resided beside the window that looked out upon the harbor. She let us play with the dollhouse, and we would carefully act out stories and plays with the dolls and furniture. We would turn on the radio in Bay's room and dance, then get out the records, put on grass *hula* skirts and sway to the music of "Little Brown Gal." Peggy would try to show me how to *hula*: "Keep your shoulders straight, swing from the hips. Joan, you're moving your shoulders. Swing from your hips down." Forgetting the blackouts and air raid drills, we would dance the afternoon away, in her sunny room above the dungeon. We were almost inseparable that summer, playing, dancing, swimming, and going to the movies.

"Gone With the Wind" came to Ford Island's base theater. We were all there transfixed, unmindful of its length. The war scenes of the injured men crowding the hospital and lying by the train station in flaming Atlanta stunned us. I had read the novel while curled on the flowered covered chaise lounge on the *lanai* after Mother had finished it. Bonnie's death, falling from her horse as she attempted the jumps, saddened me. I worried that they'd left one of Scarlett's other children out of the movie. How could the story be complete when one of the characters had been left out of the script? "Why?" I asked Mother later.

I remember her gentle answer: "But then the movie would have been so much longer. Sometimes we don't get the whole story."

A few weeks after seeing the movie, we received bad news. Janice Pritchard, our oldest friend, was leaving Hawaii. The thought of losing her was hard to imagine.

Janice called Peggy with the news that her father had been ordered back to the mainland. "Girls, put on your blue suspender wool skirts today and your white blouses," Mother told us. "I want to take pictures of you, Janice, and her house before we go down to the ship to see her off."

Peggy and I were dressed alike again, and somehow it was nice to know that we could still be alike. Peggy was getting taller. She could not cross the suspenders across her back like she used to do, but I still could. We stood in front of the tree in the Pritchards' front yard with Janice, holding arms crisscrossed and smiling. Then we went down to the Aloha Tower while she and her family boarded the ship. They threw the rainbow-colored strands of paper to us on the dock, and Mother took pictures as the ship slowly pulled away. The band was playing "Aloha Oe" for goodbye, and we were very sad.

Mother was much sadder. Her laugh was missing again, her face drawn with worry. "They are going back to the mainland. They'll be safe," she said quietly as we drove home. "I wish we were going too."

Peggy and I glanced at each other and looked away. Safe from what? I couldn't ask.

When we got home that day and went to put our skirts on hangers, Mother came into our room and asked for them. "I want them to be clean and neat for when you need them next," she explained. I didn't know what they needed to be cleaned for. We only wore them once a year now for special events, and I didn't think we'd be wearing them soon again. Later I saw Mother packing them, newly cleaned, in boxes. I didn't realize then that she was, again, getting ready.

Summer was drawing to a close. It was a "clean the pool" day, a nothing-much-to-do day. All the children met in front of Quarters A, Tommy and Jimmy Shoemaker's quarters, deciding what to do.

We began looking at the fruit on the ground. I don't remember who picked up the first mango and threw it, but suddenly the cry went up, "Mango War, boys against the girls." We began tossing the overripe fruit, juices flowing down our arms, big splats on our bodies and sun suits where the pulpy fruit hit. We soon ran out of ripe mangoes, so we picked the green ones off the trees. They were harder but we didn't care: this was war.

Finally, out of ready weapons, we looked at the littered ground. What had we done! Piles of shredded, mashed mangoes littered the street and lawn in front of Captain Shoemaker's home, and he was the executive officer of the island! Guilt assailed us. We scoured the street and ground, picking up the debris, trying to erase the evidence, pledging each other to absolute secrecy. No one was to say a word.

The next day Peggy and I began to itch. A strange rash that oozed yellow goop appeared on our arms and body. Unable to stop itching and play, we called Bay and told her.

Bay, who along with all the other children for some reason had escaped the symptoms, listened to us and solemnly gave her diagnosis, "Mango Rash. It's caused by the juice of an unripe mango. Don't tell your mother how you got it, or we'll all be in trouble. I heard my father telling my mother that all the mangos on our end of the island have disappeared."

"What has happened to you girls?" asked our mother. "What have you been into?" By this time the rash had spread from head to foot. We could hardly see out of the narrow slits that had become our eyes. Peggy certainly didn't look like a "queen" anymore. We denied any knowledge of what had caused our condition. Mother took us into the dispensary at two o'clock in the morning; the doctor prescribed oatmeal baths. We bathed in the cold water, the clumps of oatmeal bobbing like boats in the bathtub.

"How did you girls get this?" Mother asked again and again.

"We don't know, we just don't know." Our lips were sealed about the Mango War. Peggy and I had told the doctor our rehearsed story. "We were alone when we saw mangoes on the tree. We picked them off to eat them." We thought everyone believed us, since no other children on the island had the rash. We itched in silence.

Finally, several days later when we were healing and able to go out, Mother took us for a walk. "How are the girls?" asked the mother next door in Quarters S. "They look much better. Did they tell you how they got the rash?"

We rushed Mother off, Peggy pleading that she felt a little sick, before there was too much talking, but not before I heard the word, "mangoes." When school opened the following week for the fall semester, Mrs. Ulner announced that the Kenneth Whiting School Board had declared that in the future unripe mangoes were not to picked from the trees. We children kept straight faces as we listened, but, after all, that was an easy rule to follow now, since there were so few mangoes left.

Peggy and I were in the same class in September, Mrs. Baread's fifth-sixth combination class. I didn't like being in the same class with Peggy; we had already begun fighting at home. May Day and the kiss had led us on different paths, and we solved our differences with scratching, kicking, and pulling hair. We were pretty evenly matched. Peggy was strong. I was wiry. Our truces were uneasy.

"This fighting has got to stop," Mother commanded after a particularly fierce battle between Peggy and me, which included dodging, kicking, and hair pulling. "You can't fight like animals any more. If you're going to fight, you'll have to follow the rules of boxing." Now, Peggy and I knew all about boxing. We'd been following the career of Daddy's station wagon driver. We had cheered his successes and commiserated at his losses. But we were not prepared for Mother's next action.

"This will be the ring," she said, pacing off an area on our green Chinese carpet between the couch and the stone fireplace in the living room. "No kicking, scratching, hitting below the belt or hair pulling." She rang the bronze Chinese bell that Daddy had bought in China.

I did not expect Peggy to sock me in my mouth with her first punch. My mouth bled. I tested my teeth with my tongue; my two permanent front teeth now moved back and forth. Later I talked to Mother, demonstrating the wiggle. "If you fight, you may get hurt," Mother replied, handing me a tissue and turning her attention to the book she'd been reading.

So Peggy and I kept a strained peace on the home front and took our discord to school. Mrs. Baread had started the semester off by stationing a big corkboard with carefully marked vertical strips at the front of the room where we could all see it. "We're going on the demerit system now," Mrs. Baread announced. "You children will start off with one hundred merits. Should a student misbehave, I will cut off merits." She held up a big black pair of scissors and demonstrated with a snipping motion, click, click, click.

Mrs. Baread had been Peggy's teacher the previous year. She liked Peggy and often left her in charge of the class. One fateful day early in the fall of 1941, she

48

announced, "Now, Peggy Ann, if anyone says even one word, I want you to write his or her name down." She handed Peggy her black class book and left the room. I had a feeling this could be trouble.

The whispering started the moment the teacher left the room. Words flew around my ears. Peggy did not write any names down. Mother had sent me to school with cough drops for a sore throat. I took one out.

"Psst, Joan, can I have a cough drop?"

I didn't answer.

"Could you give me one?" asked Tommy.

"No," I said softly.

Peggy raised her voice, "Joan, you're talking. I'm going to report you." She wrote my name down in the book. She whispered to Mrs. Baread upon her return, showing her my name, the only one on the page. Out came the scissors, click, click, click, click. Off came four merits. I pushed my teeth with my tongue and felt them move.

Mother did go to school to plead my case: "The girls are not getting along well right now. This seems to be one demonstration. Please put the merits back."

Mrs. Baread tacked the merits back with a straight pin, alluding all the while to the dire things she planned to do to my citizenship grade. I was not assuaged, because my vertical strip now had a pin in it for all the world to see. Peggy's and my battle lines were drawn.

And then everyone's attention was diverted when Daddy announced that the school was going to hold a Court Martial. In June of 1941, Daddy was given an additional duty on Ford Island: Senior Member of the Kenneth Whiting School Board. We didn't know exactly what his responsibilities were, but, in September of 1941, Don, a sixth grade boy from Pearl City, played hooky, taking a group of fellow students into Honolulu for the day instead of catching the launch to school. The school board opted to hold a mock military Court Martial, determining that it was one thing if Don wanted to skip school by himself, but quite another matter since he chose to take several younger students with him.

I liked Don, who was two years older than I was. We shared the same birthday, December 29. Maybe I even had a crush on him. "But nothing happened to them," I said to Daddy. "They got home safely."

"Joan, you know that we all have to follow orders. Don did not, and he endangered the younger children."

I should have known better. You didn't argue with Daddy when he felt so strongly about safety and duty.

The Court Martial took place on the lanai of Kenneth Whiting School, where we usually took our rest period. All the chairs from all the classrooms were set up in rows for the children to sit in. All of us had to be present, perhaps forty of us. The *lanai*, where we used to rest and have quiet dreams, now looked forbidding. We sat up straight in our wooden chairs, trying not to move or tip them, trying not to make a sound. The Court Martial Board, comprised of all the school board members, sat at a long table at the front of the room. The defendants, Don and the other miscreants, sat in a separate area to the right of the table; they were allowed defense representation by adult spokespersons.

The charges against Don were read: "He willfully took a group of children into Honolulu, against orders, and thus endangered them." Don admitted guilt. He was found guilty as charged, and the sentence was read: "Don is hereby expelled from Kenneth Whiting School. He is to remove all his personal effects from the classroom immediately." The gavel pounded down, bringing order to the *lanai*, and the voice, not Daddy's (for which I was secretly grateful), continued, "Now we

50

will consider the lesser charges of 'Absent Without Leave' for the students who accompanied him."

Don left the *lanai*, heading into the classroom to remove his things. I followed. He would now have to go to school in Honolulu, probably fall behind, and be retained a year when he went back to the mainland. The two of us were standing alone by Mrs. Baread's desk. Don's head was lowered and a shock of his dirty blond hair covered his face so I could not see him cry.

The other students were subsequently placed under "house arrest." They couldn't leave their quarters without their parents. It was a sad day, but we were soon to be reminded at school about "following orders" and "discharging our duties."

Air raid drills, which had become almost routine at home, now in early October came to Kenneth Whiting School.

"When the siren blasts up and down, you are to leave the school building and get on the buses outside," Mrs. Uhler sternly ordered. "This is not a fire drill. You must move quickly and quietly." The siren wailed. We followed orders and boarded the buses, after which we were driven about half a mile over to the dispensary, supposedly safer because it was a hospital. We waited there quietly until the "all clear" sounded and the buses returned us back to the school. We were learning the rules of survival in war.

Along with the drills, everyone on the island had to get Yellow Fever shots. We took our turns down at the dispensary: two shots, the one in the soft part of each upper arm. The one on my right arm swelled up into a bright red spot two inches in diameter. We children compared our shots and different sizes of swellings at the swimming pool. Mine was the largest, and it hurt. I thought I should get a medal for valor. I said so to Mother, but she wasn't paying much attention to us.

She had larger worries on her mind. Peggy and I heard her talking to Daddy late at night, her voice agitated. "Dolph, we must send the girls home, home to New Jersey. You sister Maude will take care of them."

"You're getting too upset," Daddy's voice was soothing. "The girls are safe here."

"No, I had the dream again. They are in danger. We must send them back to the mainland."

Peggy and I listened from our bedroom. Something strange was happening in our house. What was the dream about? How could we not be safe with the ships to guard us? We knew Mother had been packing sealed boxes with our names printed on them in Daddy's workshop. I asked Mother what the boxes were for.

"Clothing and bedding for you and Peggy. I want to have things ready. We may have to leave in a hurry," Mother explained.

Peggy and I talked that night about the air raid drill at school. If an attack were to come while we were at school, we wouldn't be with Mother. A war was coming. I knew it was coming. They had dug pits over by the airfield for gun emplacements, but they hadn't put the guns in yet.

How big would the newspaper headlines be when we were attacked? We visualized the page in our minds as Peggy and I talked in the night. The Adventure Girls were meeting in Bay Bellinger's dungeon in the morning. It was time to make a few plans of our own.

Six

Peggy and I rode our bikes the next morning for the meeting in Bay's dungeon. We stopped at the top of the circular driveway that led down to the entrance of the fort. The air was crystal clear. I felt I could see forever as I looked at the harbor, the sugar cane fields beyond, then the mountains meeting the clear blue sky. We could see the ships peacefully at anchor in the harbor, the launches skittering across the sapphire water: the startling clarity of power and peace.

We parked our bikes at the entrance to the dungeon, met Bay, and waited for the other girls to arrive. We sat on the cold concrete floor of our play area; the morning sun had yet to warm the air. One overhead light chased away the shadows. Finally everyone else arrived for the meeting.

Although our names were duly recorded in Peggy's Composition book, we had not yet heard of *Robert's Rules of Order* explaining how a meeting should be run. We seemed to all talk at once, sharing one common idea: we had to get ready. We knew the attack was going to come.

"There aren't enough places for people to sit in this room," declared Bay.

We all agreed, since, based on drills we'd been through, we knew we'd have to plan for at least fifty adults and children.

"Peggy and I can bring over our two chairs," I replied. "The child-sized wooden chairs with green and white plaid padding on the seats. The ones we got for Easter, 1939, when we lived on Yerba Buena in San Francisco Bay."

"We need to have something for children to drink," interjected Bay. "Something more than the water in the bathroom." She was referring to the small bathroom on the right hand side of the dungeon in the biggest, round gun emplacement that up to now we had called the "forbidden room."

"We'll need aprons to put over our clothes," offered Ann Dale.

"Good idea," Peggy answered. "We'll bring over our pinafores."

The Adventure Girls' Club became somber. We would serve lemonade and fudge during the attack to everyone in the shelter. Chairs would be brought from our homes for additional seating. Peggy and I would bring over our pinafores, and other girls would bring their aprons. Each of us would have a job. We would begin our preparations that day. Peggy, I, and the rest would all make fudge at home to have it ready. We left the meeting with resolve.

Peggy and I approached Mother. I spoke. "We want to take our Easter chairs over to the shelter. We're making fudge tonight. Our club is going to help when the attack comes." As of that date, we ceased to call our clubhouse the "dungeon;" we now referred to it as the "shelter."

Mother looked at me strangely. She was quiet for a very long time. When she spoke, there was something new in her voice. It sounded like respect. "You're getting ready."

So then we finally knew what "getting ready" meant. We took the chairs over, balancing them on the handlebars of our bicycles. We carried our pinafores over on hangers. We felt prepared.

The boys were making their own plans. They were building a fort in the empty gun emplacement that had been dug near Luke Field. Tommy and Jimmy pulled pieces of cardboard across the top and climbed in and out on a ladder. They were our age, but we wondered how they could be so dumb. "That's not a safe place to be during the attack," we advised them.

They didn't listen to us.

Peggy and I went home to watch Daddy on his new building project: a back yard barbecue, made out of big gray concrete blocks. He and a few of his Marines labored over the construction. We'd been in Hawaii a year, and it was time for Peggy's eleventh birthday, October 18, 1941. A dozen or more boys and girls had been invited to her party. Mother's job was to catch the ferry, drive into Honolulu, and bring back the birthday cake.

Mother arrived back at one o'clock with a box, which she opened. She then placed on the kitchen counter an astonishing cake, a large white round layer cake maybe fifteen inches across and decorated with violet flowers growing on delicate green vines and supported by a chocolate trellis. "Happy 11th Birthday, Peggy Ann" swirled across the top in chocolate letters.

"Oh! It's the most beautiful cake I've ever seen!" Peggy exclaimed.

The front doorbell rang; it was Daddy's driver. "Mother, can I show him the cake?" she asked.

"Yes, but be careful."

Peggy lifted the cake off the counter and walked out through the dining room. Her foot caught on the edge of the small green Chinese throw rug. She -- and the cake, of course -- fell in the dining room entry.

The cake splattered all over the dining room's hardwood floor and the rug. Parts of the frosted top landed upside down creating a mosaic of violet, green, white, and chocolate globules. Peggy dissolved into tears and ran into the living room, where Mother and Daddy followed, trying to comfort her. I could hear them talking in soft voices.

There was not enough time to go into Honolulu for another cake. I walked into the dining room and began picking up the parts of the cake, fitting them together like pieces of a puzzle. I carried the thing into the kitchen. Out came the butter, powdered sugar, vanilla, and yellow food coloring. I blended a new frosting in a bowl. With a spatula I carefully spread the frosting, trying to camouflage the cracks.

"Look, Peggy!" I announced, carrying the now yellow cake into the living room. Nobody spoke as they gazed in amazement. "We can keep the dining room lights off. Maybe they won't notice much in the dim light."

The three of them gathered around my revised cake as it sat on the Chinese chow bench. Peggy's tears dried. I knew my father was proud of my cake repair work. But my mother paid no heed to my salvage job. "Dolph," she said, "their lives are as fragile as the lattice work on the cake."

Daddy looked at her gently, then turned and said to us, "We'll serve the cake late in the afternoon, when the ships sound retreat."

Later that evening, when the last guest had left, Mother and Daddy gave Peggy her present. She opened the small white box, took out a white enclosure, and there on a silk backing was a Marine Corps emblem with a gold chain connecting it to a signature pin. She loved it.

I did too. " Oh, I want one too!"

"Now, Joan, you know we never give presents ahead of time. You'll have to wait until your birthday. It's only two months away."

"Mother, I have the feeling that if I don't get one now, I'll never get one. Something tells me my birthday will be too late."

Mother looked at me, that strange look again on her face. Daddy listened. The next evening a little white envelope, closed in the middle by a snap, was by my plate.

In my memory, on November 12, 1941 our family enacted another evening air raid drill: we imagined a siren going off, and our family of four ran the three blocks to the shelter. We stood in the room until we pretended to hear the steady blast of the all clear signal that told us we could go home. We were getting proficient at the rules of war.

Two weeks later, I was on the *lanai* reading when I heard Mother and Daddy talking as they dressed for the Thanksgiving Dance.

"I don't like the idea of talks with the Japanese," Daddy said. "I don't believe what the radio and newspapers say. I meant what I said in New Jersey: the Japanese are aggressive. I saw it in China, and I'm seeing it now."

"It's too late, now, to send the girls back," Mother replied. In her long floral black linen dress, she looked like a young girl. Her short white jacket was bordered with appliqués echoing the dress's yellow and white daisies. She weighed ninety pounds and looked fragile. Her face, even with extra makeup, had about it the dazed look of someone who'd seen a ghost.

Daddy looked his handsome self in his white dress uniform. He towered over Mother, but they made a dramatic couple. Peggy and I begged them to have their picture taken at the party. The photograph is standing now in its frame on my piano. Two smiling faces caught in time.

Peggy, I, and the rest of the Ford Island children were learning a dance of our own, the *hula*. We were practicing for a Hawaiian Festival at Kenneth Whiting School. Originally planned for the end of November, it had been postponed for two weeks due to a heavy flow of "liquid sunshine." It had rained so hard that Peggy and I had encountered waist-deep puddles on the way to school.

The rain didn't stop any of the fathers from going to the Army Navy Game Party at the Officers' Club behind our quarters, where they listened to the game by radio. Daddy relived the games he'd played while at the Academy; he became hoarse from cheering. We could hear the yells in our quarters as Navy won the 1941 game. I have thought over the years that, had the Japanese planned an attack that day, our base's response might have been even slower.

Sunday, November 30th, the rain had stopped, and the weather suddenly turned warm. Daddy and Colonel Davidson decided to take their families boating in the harbor. Mrs. Davidson, Sally, her brother, and Peggy and I climbed gingerly onto the sailboat tied up at the dock adjacent to the aircraft carriers. My mother wasn't going. Because of her fair skin, she had to avoid the sun. Besides, she seemed very preoccupied now.

"Sir," a seaman, his back ramrod straight and a bit of a quaver in his voice, addressed Daddy, "this boat doesn't have a jib. You may have trouble steering her."

"When I was fourteen, I sailed boats on the Hudson River. I can handle it all right," Daddy replied. Colonel Davidson appeared equally confident.

But almost immediately after we left the dock and were out in the harbor, the boat began to heel over in the water. It yawed drastically from side to side. We children were instructed to move our weight around to compensate. "This boat's going to turn over!" yelled Mrs. Davidson. "Get down in the cabin, children."

But I knew we'd drown if we went down in the cabin. How would we be able to get out when the boat turned over? Mrs. Davidson was adamant, commanding us to go down into the bowels of the boat, so we did. My stomach began to cramp as I thought about how the water would feel as we sank. I don't know how many minutes went by. It seemed like hours. Finally, Mrs. Davidson let us back crawl out as the boat somehow approached the dock.

But even as Daddy tried to get the boat back into the dock, we were in trouble. He tried five times, but without a jib the boat would not be steered.

"Here, ahoy there," a voice boomed. We looked up. The deck of the *U.S.S. Enterprise* was lined with sailors, their faces tiny because they were perhaps fifty feet above us looking down. "We'll send out a boat," the amplified voice from above continued.

We were towed into shore, having been rescued by an aircraft carrier.

Later that evening after the Davidsons left, I walked across the grass in front of Quarters T, down the little path to the water. I sat watching the ships, hearing the bells and the piping of the boatswain's whistle. I watched and waved to the men on board, and they waved back. I sat, warmed by the sun low in the sky, safe in the shadow of our ships.

Seven

We were singing the song we had practiced for weeks:

> It's not the islands fair
>   that are calling to me
> It's not the balmy air
>   nor the tropical sea
> It's a little brown gal
>   in a little grass skirt
> In a little grass shack
>   in Hawaii

Friday, December 5, 1941. We were dancing the hula in the Hawaiian Festival at Kenneth Whiting School. The shadow of the *Oklahoma's* mast bisected the grassy playground as our tanned bodies swayed to the music. We had been practicing the hula for months, ever since we'd started our club with Ann Dale O'Brien, Bay Bellinger, and Margaret Grant.

"Hold your shoulders straight and swing from the waist, not with your whole body. Rotate your hips, move with light steps forward and backward to the music, turn around smoothly in small circles."

I repeated the directions under my breath as I gazed sideways at Peggy, checking my movements with hers. I knew she could wiggle better than I could. But I danced, waving my hand softly sideways to imitate the breezes, hands moving gently down my sides for the skirt, sweaty fingers tented for the hut.

We were all browned from the days of sun. Our feet had hardened by walking barefoot. We wore hibiscus leis around our necks and hibiscus flowers in our hair. We were no longer *haoles*, newcomers, but *kama'ainas*, oldtimers, on Ford Island. I was a nine year-old little brown girl in a little grass skirt in Hawaii.

My schoolmates took turns on the small raised latticework stage, telling the tales of Maui. Retelling the legends. How Maui strung the islands together for a necklace that broke and formed an unlinked chain. Peggy told how Maui had attempted to halt the sun with a rope braided of strands of hair from faithful maidens. One maiden had not been faithful, so the rope had broken and now only slowed the sun.

I told the story of Pele, Goddess of the Fire. When Pele was angry the volcanoes would explode. She must be appeased. The priests would sound a gong to warn the people that the wise men were looking for someone to throw into the volcano. Everyone would hide until the human sacrifice had been found; a second signal would announce an "all clear" indicating that the search had been successful. Then everyone would come out from hiding and rejoice that Pele was now happy and the volcanoes' eruptions would stop.

Mother and Daddy watched along with the other parents on the sun-drenched playground. Our voices filled the air as we closed the festival with "Aloha Oe," singing in Hawaiian and in English:

> Aloha oe, aloha oe,
> Eke ona o no no hoi ha lipo
> One fond embrace, aho i a eau
> Until we meet again.

I sang with all my heart. I knew "aloha oe" meant both hello and goodbye. I did not realize that we were singing goodbye. We would not meet at Kenneth Whiting School again.

The next morning, the Adventure Girls met once more in the dungeon -- now the air raid shelter -- in the basement of Admiral Bellinger's quarters. We went over the rules for getting to the shelter that we'd been practicing since March. We discussed our plans to serve lemonade and fudge during the attack. We tried on our pinafores. We sat in the chairs we'd brought over from Quarters T for people to use during the attack.

Our meeting was interrupted when the boys came over to taunt us. "Our fort is better than yours," they chanted.

We charged out calling, "Catch us if you can!"

We spied on them; they chided and yelled. We retaliated by storming their club, climbing down the ladder into the hole that had been dug for a gun. It was boys versus girls all morning.

Suddenly there was dissention in our group; we girls began to argue. Words flew through the air. The boys kept teasing. The situation escalated; there was no hope of peace. In a huff of bad temper, we broke up the club. The boys were only too happy to help Peggy and me take our chairs back to Quarters T, balancing them on the handlebars of their bikes.

Peggy and I trudged home, clutching our pinafores in our hands, knowing in our hearts that we had to make peace with Bay so we'd still be able to help people during the attack. But we mentally excused ourselves temporarily, thinking we had enough time. We decided that that night would be a great time to camp out in the back yard with our new compatriots, the boys.

"Daddy, we want to join the boys' club. We want to sleep in pup tents in the backyard. It'll be fun. Please, Daddy?" we entreated as my father sat in the living room listening to his short wave radio.

Daddy shushed me, frowning as he held his finger to his lips. I could hear the radio announcers' words, "Japanese," "Washington D.C.," "meeting scheduled for tomorrow." He turned to me, his face relaxing into a smile. "No, not tonight, Joan. Tomorrow's a big day. We have church in the morning, the trip to the aquarium in Honolulu, and then dinner. No, no, not tonight."

Peggy and I pleaded a little more, but he wouldn't budge. The boys left. We spent the evening reading and watching the chrysalis of a big green caterpillar that we'd captured in the backyard and placed in a large jar. There had been no movement at all for the past several days; that meant it was time for him to emerge. When would it happen, we wondered. We had happy thoughts for tomorrow, said "sweet dreams," and went to bed.

My sister and I woke up early that Sunday morning. Mother called us, still wearing our lightweight seersucker nighties, into her room, "Girls, we have to have the pork roast in the oven at eight o'clock when the ships raise the 'colors.' Joan, please peel the onions. Peggy, you have the job of chopping onions. I'll come out and put it in when I hear the bugle sounding "prep" at 7:55."

Peggy and I knew that "raising the colors" meant putting up the flag, after which the ships would then toll eight bells. We'd never needed clocks in Quarters T; the ships were our timekeepers.

The uncooked pork roast was lying on the table in the center of the kitchen, the breadboard for chopping the onions beside it. Peeling onions wasn't as bad as

64

chopping, I thought, but I did hold the onions under the running water in the sink, trying not to cry, while I peeled off the skins. My mission accomplished, I started walking out of the kitchen and into the lanai.

"Help me," Peggy commanded to my retreating back.

"No!" I replied. "I've already peeled them. Besides, there's not very much to chop."

I wanted to do what I liked best, to curl up and read on the chaise lounge, to settle in, feeling the warmth of the cushions. I'd just finished reading and "raising" *Jo's Boys* and was disgusted that Louisa Mae Alcott hadn't written any more books about the March family. After searching the Kenneth Whiting School library, I'd finally found her *Under the Lilacs* and was deeply engrossed in the story of Bab and Betty. They were the same age as Peggy and I and were having a tea party under the lilacs in their yard.

Peggy was mad at me for not helping. She was at the bread board, slamming the chopper down, thump, thump, thump, trying to make me feel guilty. I didn't feel guilty. I drowned her out, concentrating my eyes on the page.

Then, suddenly, out of the corner of my eye I saw a grayish-black column of smoke. Something was burning. I dropped the book and ran out the lanai door to look.

Fire! There! Over the row of hibiscus bushes towards Luke Field I saw fire! Smoke and flames rose, filling the sky with a black cloud. It looked like the water tower was on fire! How could the water tower be on fire? It was made out of metal! "Run!" my brain ordered. "Run back inside the quarters. Tell Mother."

"Mother, the water tower's on fire!" I announced, standing in the doorway of her room.

She was sitting in her bed, her nightgown clad body turned, her face looking out the windows, ignoring my soft voice, saying, "Why are those puffs of smoke rising off the *West Virginia*? Why are we having gunnery practice on Sunday morning?"

Mother was not listening to me! She could only see ahead towards the ships. Why were the ships firing guns? What was happening out front? I turned and ran out the front door to see what was causing the puffs of smoke. Just then, a strange plane with red balls on the sides of its body swooped low over my head, diving towards the masts of the *West Virginia* and *Tennessee*. What plane was that? What was it doing flying so low?

I ran, ran, back into the house, back to my mother's bedroom. It was empty! Run, run, to Daddy's room. Mother and Daddy, still in his pajamas, were standing facing each other, framing the window with their bodies, talking, gesturing. I spoke louder this time. "The water tower's on fire, and a strange plane just flew over my head."

Mother was talking to Daddy about bullets coming close to the quarters. Daddy, who had just come out of his bathroom, was saying, "They shouldn't do that in port." I heard snatches of words, "strange plane," "maneuvers on Sunday," "too low," "no identification," "forced landing."

I realized that they still were not listening to me. Now I yelled: "The water tower's on fire, and a strange plane just flew right over my head!"

They still weren't listening to me. And then, looking between them out the window, I knew something was terribly wrong. The masts of the battleships always stood strong and parallel. Now they weren't. The masts of the *West Virginia* were tilting crazily to the right!

"Look out the window!" I yelled. They weren't listening to me! "Look out the window! Please look out the window!"

Daddy turned his head to look Time stood still as his eyes took in the scene. Then he shouted, "My god, that ship is listing! It's the Japs! We're under bombardment! GET TO THE SHELTER!" He turned, picked up his uniform pants, and started to pull them on over his pajamas. He called his men on the phone, saying, "Dammit, It's the Japs."

We had our orders. Get to the shelter!

"Get your bathrobes and put them on. Find your shoes. Don't put your shoes on." Mother's directions were short and clear. "It'll take too long. Carry your shoes!"

Robes on and shoes in hand, we were ready to go.

Which door to go out? The dining room door: it was the safest, away from the ships. Run, run, get to the shelter. Peggy broke away from Mother, veering to the right in front of the Quarters S where a young boy stood staring out of the window at us. "It's real!" Peggy yelled to him, "It's real! Get to the shelter."

Mother grabbed Peggy's hand, "Stay with me!" We got to the corner where the short side street met Lexington Road. A plane was flying low, its machine guns firing, bullets flying and thudding into the ground.

"They're strafing us," Mother screamed. "Get your heads down, bend over, and run as fast as you can!"

"Get in here! Get in quick! They're shooting at you!" a voice yelled at us from the glassed in kitchen area at the rear of the BOQ. Mother raised her head and looked. Men were beckoning from the service entrance of the BOQ. "Get in here now!"

We straightened up and started to run, Mother's arms covering our heads, trying to shield us. The floor of the service entrance, where trucks ordinarily backed up to offload supplies, was three feet off the ground. How were we going to reach that high? Mother went first, the men pulling her up and into the kitchen, showing us the way we could follow. Up, up, three men pulled us, bruising Peggy's chest on the wooden threshold. We found ourselves in the large, airy BOQ kitchen, which opened into the officers' dining room. Windows extended on all three sides from the countertops to the ceiling.

"Get under something!" said a male voice. Peggy scuttled under the kitchen sink. Mother and I crawled under the large wooden kitchen table in the center of the room. Huddle, hide, we are safe for a minute, my brain recorded.

Whomp!!!!! An explosion louder than any crack of thunder or volcanic eruption shook the building, immediately followed by a rain of fire. Even from under the table where I was kneeling, I could see clearly out the kitchen windows. The familiar greenery outside the building was obliterated. On three sides, flaming material now filled the sky. Peggy could see as well from where she was crouched. The BOQ's on fire I thought. The BOQ's on fire! We're going to be trapped in here and burned up.

I'd never been a screamer, but now I became hysterical. I felt sure that the roof over our heads was already in flames. Stark terror swallowed me. I began yelling words I though I would never say, "I hate Ford Island, I hate Ford Island. I want to go back to the mainland!"

Mother, kneeling next to me, held my shaking body in her arms. For some reason, she was not screaming, nor was my sister. But I have never fully recovered from what my mother said next: "Don't cry, Joan. Don't cry. Marines don't cry. Don't ruin the morale of the men."

I stopped. After that, I turned my screams inward, becoming mute in my terror.

A sailor walked through the swinging door out of the kitchen towards the front of the building. He quickly returned ashen faced, commanding, "Nobody leaves this building. I am in charge here."

We didn't know at the time what he'd seen, but of course I now know it was the *Arizona* engulfed in flames.

Waiting, waiting, under the table, I sat mute as the Japanese planes flew directly over us..

Suddenly a Marine climbed up through the service entrance, the same one we'd used, a bayoneted rifle in his hands. He looked at Mother in her bathrobe huddled in the kitchen of the BOQ. He evidently thought at first that she had spent the night. "You ought to be ashamed of yourself!" Then he saw Peggy and me huddling under the sink and table. He recognized that he was addressing the wife of his C.O. and he began apologizing, "I'm sorry, Mrs. Zuber. I didn't know it was you. I'll have to get you out of here. I'm taking you and the girls to the shelter."

We moved quickly out from under our meager protection, and he lifted us back out onto the ground. Then he lifted my sister and me into the cab of a waiting truck. My mother climbed in next, and he hurried around to the driver's side. An armed Marine sat behind us in the open truck bed. We careened down the road.

As we passed the BOQ, I looked to the right and saw a ship low in the water, completely covered in flames that reached the sky. What ship was that? I realized with wonder that I could now not recognize which ship it was. The sight etched itself in my mind, never to be forgotten. We turned left, heading for Admiral Bellinger's quarters. The truck stopped, and we ran down the driveway into our dungeon/playground/ shelter.

"Here, inside here. You are among the last to arrive," a uniformed man said to us. He pushed us into the open gun emplacement area just inside the door. We put our shoes on and stood, the whole vista of the harbor spread out before us through the gun emplacement opening.

We could see the *Solace*, the hospital ship, with its red cross sitting out in the middle of the harbor, rocking from side to side from the force of the bombs hitting the water. Small boats carrying wounded were racing out to her. Geysers of water exploded as dropped bombs missed what seemed to us to be their apparent target -- the hospital ship. Overhead, Japanese planes flew high and low.

We and the others in the open room cheered, "They've missed. The *Solace* is still safe."

I could not count the number of women and children in the room. I only knew that around us, on the floor, and leaning against the concrete walls, were the bodies of the wounded. One man was screaming in pain, black oil coating his stark red burns, his skin shedding off his arms.

It was a good thing, I thought, that we children had fought yesterday and taken our little chairs home: now there was more room for the causalities to lie prone.

One older sailor, his skin flayed off in palm-sized strips, bravely looked at us young children and said with both astonishment and distress, "What are these children doing in here, seeing this?"

New orders came. We had to move; the adults were afraid that bullets would come into the open emplacement. "Walk with your eyes straight ahead directly on the person in front of you. Do not look to the sides." I obeyed, but the cries and moans of the wounded men, as they lay lining the walls, filled my ears.

Peggy looked, then gasped and said, "I want to help them. Oh, how I wish I could help them."

I felt the same way, but I said nothing.

We were now in what had been the forbidden room, the one in the dungeon that was always kept closed, and from which we could sometimes see the servants coming and going. The door was open now. We entered into a large room with at least four twin-sized beds. It was crowded with dependants -- sitting, standing, crying, and vomiting, but with no visible wounds. There were only a few high windows in the room. We could no longer see outside; now we could only see each other.

The mother and the little boy from Quarters S were already in the room. Peggy was relieved that this woman had made it to the shelter. One man had brought his family. I scorned him, thinking that Daddy had gone instead to his men. I was proud of Daddy.

Peggy and I sat back to back on one of the beds. This was what war was. I stood, my mind taking pictures, snap, snap, snap. This was war.

Tommy asked Peggy, "Do you think they bombed the school?"

First Sergeant's wife was weeping, not for her husband but for the men.

Mrs. Bellinger was helping out with the men.

Mother was comforting a little girl who thought her kitten had been killed, saying, "I read about the care of pets in England during the air raids. It said to do as much for dogs as possible and never to worry about cats. They are the first ones to get under cover and the last ones to come out." The girl stopped crying.

I waited, watched mutely, my head full of unasked questions. Where was Daddy?

Was he still alive?

Mother moved around soothing the others. We girls had been right about one thing: there was nothing to drink. The water supply to the island had been cut off. Nothing trickled out of the faucets, the toilet in the bathroom had overflowed, and vomit and sewage covered the floor. Mother took charge, kneeling down on the tiles, using newspapers to sop up the mess, trying to bring order in the middle of a war.

A man entered the room, clothes disheveled, hair mussed, asking in rushed words, "Does anyone have any extra clothing? All the rags, towels, and clothes in the Bellingers' quarters have been used up. The wounded men need bandages and dressings."

Peggy and I looked down at our newly washed seersucker bathrobes. We looked at Mother. She nodded. We slipped off the robes and gave them to the man. "They will soak up the oil," Peggy said, pleased that we had found a way to help.

I waited, standing now mute, waiting for word of Daddy. My mind was numb. I could not think past the sky of fire. The "all-clear" sounded. Why? Why, I wondered. Why hadn't the air raid siren gone off? It was supposed to go off! But now we heard the "all clear."

A Marine arrived, his duty to take us back to our quarters. "Where is Daddy?" Peggy asked for all three of us. "Is he alive? Does he know we're alive?" The answer was, "Yes." My heart swelled: we had all survived, at least so far.

We walked outside the dungeon door, out into the level area of the Bellingers' driveway, before the slight grade that led up to the road. There was now a five-foot high hill of miscellaneous soiled clothes in the driveway. I looked at the pile and recognized the soft floral pattern of my bathrobe. Reaching down, I picked it up, thinking I could take it home and wash it. It was not a bathrobe; it was a five inch oily square of material. I dropped it back into the hill of used bandages.

We walked home, not talking, going home towards the flames. Turning towards the harbor, we saw the new view from Quarters T. The battleships were broken.

They lay like shattered toys in a sea of burning oil. I recognized the burning ship now. It was the *Arizona*, her tattered flag still flying on a rope by her stern, her broken mast bowed as if in prayer. Flames surrounded her.

A Marine walked by as we approached Battleship Row and home. "Do you want to see the dead Jap pilot out front?" he asked. "His plane crashed in the harbor and they pulled his body up to the grass."

We looked at Mother for permission. She nodded, yes.

The pilot was lying in the grass fifty feet in front of Quarters T. His arms were flung out, his face turned to the side. I scanned his body, searching for his wound. I couldn't find it. Peggy gestured with her finger, pointing and directing my attention to a splotch of blood on his chest, where, according to the Marine, he had been bayoneted in the heart.

This was the enemy. I wanted to kick him. The enemy lay amidst the exploded pieces of the *Arizona*. Metal, glass, forks, knives, and plate decking were his final resting place. The Marine was talking to Mother.

"There was another body there," he said. "We removed it." I looked at the cement path. There was no blood, but it was wet.

The Marine saw my look. "We washed the blood off. We were afraid it would frighten the girls," he said to Mother, answering my unspoken question. I decided not to touch the path; I would not go in through the front door.

I walked across the lawn to the back of Quarters T. As I walked, I picked up pieces of tile from the deck of the ship. I harvested the bullets, bomb fragments, small twisted pieces of metal, and a piece of tempered glass, ten inches long by one and one-half inches wide long and one inch thick, completely blackened and burnt, that had blown off the ship.

The path we'd taken as we fled out the dining room door was now bisected by a four- by ten-foot piece of plate metal buried two feet deep into the ground: a ten-foot guillotine slicing through our escape route. Mother's kimono was still hanging on the clothes line where she'd hung it on Saturday. I touched it, felt its new weight, and extricated from its pocket a three-inch piece of jagged shrapnel. I added the shrapnel to my collection.

The quarters were still standing. There was now one of our machine guns mounted on the roof. An ugly gray cylinder by the lanai door was an unexploded Japanese bomb. Inside, all the walls and ceilings were speckled with holes. Every nail used to build Quarters T had been blasted completely through the walls by the percussion from the exploding *Arizona*.

"One-half hour to get everything you need," the Marine announced. What did we need? What did we need? I tried to think of what I needed, but I didn't ask. I could not think past the ship of fire. I needed nothing.

The Marine drove us to our new air-raid shelter, the new BOQ. I knew that the Japs were coming back. They were coming back, and we had no ships and no planes with which to stop them. Maybe we had a few meager guns like the one on our roof.

"This is how you load a machine gun," the seaman explained to me that afternoon. I was sitting in the sunny concrete area in front of the new BOQ. I watched and listened carefully to his instructions. I picked up the long tapered bullets and slid them carefully into the machine gun magazine, slanting them slightly as directed. I was helping fight the enemy. I felt nothing. I said nothing. I was an automaton.

Peggy sat beside me loading gun-belts. "Every six bullets, then a tracer," she chanted under her breath. We loaded ammunition all afternoon.

There was no water on Ford Island. The water line lay under the *Arizona*; it was no more, crushed by her sunken hull. Mother was absent from us. She was with the men, using her first aid. We had not yet seen Daddy.

"Your father is alive and well," a Marine told us. "He's setting up field kitchens and three thousand cots for the men who've lost their ships, those who are still alive. He wants you to know he will come as soon as he feels we are ready and safe."

Peggy put down her bullets and looked at him. My heart gave a little leap, my mouth a sign of happiness. "Tell him that we're doing our jobs," I said as I put another bullet into the magazine. We were Marines, following orders.

The day marched slowly into evening. We were assigned a room in the BOQ, sharing it with another family. Mother was worried about the other children in our room: one was a six-year old boy who walked in his sleep. If he sleepwalked out of the building, he might be shot. The younger boy, we were to discover over the next two days, wet his bed.

We stood in the cafeteria line for food and pineapple juice. Then we talked quietly as night came. Complete blackout. The blackout was not going to do us any good, I thought. We couldn't turn off the burning *Arizona*. Her flames were a beacon signal in the night.

Suddenly the air raid siren screamed in the night. The Japs were back! The man who was supposed to turn the siren on this morning hadn't, I thought, but he was doing it now. We heard the engines of the planes and crowded outside in the warm night air to watch. The planes came overhead.

The guns that I'd helped to load in the afternoon began firing. I felt like cheering. My bullets were helping! Tracers were lighting up the sky. Planes were being shot down and crashing. We got some this time!

The cheers began to change. Something was wrong. What else could possibly go wrong? And then there was silence.

A sad murmur swept over the crowd of watchers. These planes, they were saying, were not Japanese. They were our own, off the *U.S.S. Enterprise*. Six of them. My bullets had shot at our own planes and men.

The three of us went quietly to bed, my mother saying to all of us, "Good night, sweet dreams. Don't walk in your sleep."

But my dream was a nightmare, and when I woke up in the morning I found it was real.

Eight

I woke up slowly Monday morning, looking for our familiar bedroom. It wasn't there. In our one narrow twin bed, I tried to move my legs. I couldn't. My legs were mixed up with Peggy's and Mother's. I had had a nightmare. I had dreamt that we were attacked and that the ships had died; it couldn't be real.

The three of us lay in a strange bed in a strange building. I looked at the people in the other twin bed and on the floor, remembering. We were in the New BOQ. A window faced out towards the *U.S.S. Utah*, and in the far wall a door led into a bathroom. I unwrapped my legs and went into the bathroom.

The toilet didn't work. It wouldn't flush, and the sink would not fill up with water. I remembered, then: there was no water on Ford Island. The men were draining the swimming pools for water.

A baby began to cry from the other twin bed. There was a mother, two girls, a six-year old boy, and a baby, all sharing the room with us. They were sleeping on the floor and sharing the small bed. The boy hadn't walked in his sleep last night; he'd wet the bed instead. The room was filled with cries and the smell of the bed.

"How long will we have to stay here?" I wanted to ask Mother. I knew I couldn't whisper, because she had told us never to whisper since it was "impolite." I didn't want to hurt the other family's feelings. I finally made myself say the words softly.

"We have to stay here until the *Arizona* stops burning. The house is not safe. They're afraid that the flames from the burning oil might cross the water and come up the slope and into Quarters T," she replied just as softly. The smoke from the burning *Arizona* still filled the sky. The nightmare was real. My mind turned off.

Peggy and I had breakfast in the cafeteria. All our meals would be eaten in this room. We stood in a single line that threaded its way through the large kitchen. We carried our trays, waiting for food. Peggy was afraid.

I had never seen Peggy afraid before. "I don't want to go near that oven," she said. The huge oven was open, its door raised. We could see the flames rising from the gas burners. "I'm afraid that the oven will pull me inside," she continued. I listened to her, thinking that neither of us would ever want to be near a fire again, even a little one.

We carried our trays out into the big dining room. No one talked at the table. I did not care what was on my tray. I ate with a mechanical mouth, chewing the food, swallowing the pineapple juice. All the water had been drained from the swimming pools; all that was left to drink was canned pineapple juice.

I did not see Bay or Ann Dale or Tommy and Jimmy. We were told that Bay had left the island on a launch. I didn't know where the others were. I did know where Mother was; she was again using her first aid on the wounded. When we saw Mother at lunch, her face looked drawn, like an old lady's. There were no stories, no laughter, only people walking from here to there.

Our room was too crowded, so Peggy and I sat on the hall floor just outside our room, our backs against the wall. The hall was long and dim; the lights were kept on all day. Day was the opposite of night now: lights on during the day, all lights off at night so that the Japs would not see our building and bomb us again. We could see sunshine at the end of the hall, but there, by the room, it was not day or night. We sat in the hall, waiting for Daddy.

"Your father knows that we are safe," Mother explained. "His men have told him, but he is now the Base Defense and Internal Security Officer. He has to be sure that Ford Island and its men can defend the Naval Air Station when the Japanese come back."

"I'm grateful that your father's family in New Jersey and Aunt Peggy in Washington D.C. don't know where our quarters are," she continued. "They know we're here in Hawaii, but not exactly where. Perhaps they won't worry about us too much."

But Peggy and I worried; we worried about Daddy. We knew he was taking care of the men. She and I talked together, trying to imagine exactly where he was and what he was doing. Peggy was the one person I could still talk to.

A Marine off the West Virginia approached us, his clothes covered with oil, a result of his swim from his ship to the shore. He told us, "I saw Major Zuber down at the barracks. Thanks to him, the Parade Ground is covered with canvas tents which are sheltering cots. We're all grateful for your father." I was thankful that the young Marine had survived his flaming oil swim without injury.

The night before, the Navy father of the other family in the room had come many times during the night to check on his wife and children, using a flashlight to find his way. He'd awakened us every time.

"He's supposed to be on duty," Peggy said quietly to me as we sat in the hall. "He's putting his family before his duty. We miss Daddy, but he and we are Marines. That's the difference."

Peggy and I did not load machine guns on Monday: we sat in the hall waiting for the next time to go into the cafeteria. We could hear Mother talking to the mother of the family sharing our room. The little boy had wet the other bed during his nap. Now there was no place to sleep and no place to go.

The ferry was out of commission. The only way off Ford Island was by launch, and the launches were taking off the wounded men. We missed our playmates. Where were they? Maybe their quarters were not in so much danger. Maybe they were able to go home and sleep in their own beds.

Kenneth Whiting School was closed. A bomb had dropped into the middle of the playground, but it was a "dud." No damage was done. We were learning new words: a "dud" was an unexploded bomb which had to be removed by special people. But Mrs. Uhler had come over by boat from the Pearl City Peninsula late Sunday evening to inspect the school. She saw the capsized *Oklahoma* and the bodies on the shore by the launch landing. "The school is in no condition to open. The children mustn't come back here. There is too much death." She declared the school closed.

A delayed-action bomb had landed on the dispensary. Daddy was there at the time, and was cut by falling glass. The injury was minor; he refused treatment.

Mother handed Peggy and me blankets as we sat in the hall that night. "Girls, we'll have to sleep out here tonight. Both the beds are wet." We rolled up in the lightweight blankets, unmindful of the hard floor.

The father of the family in our room came in with his flashlight during the night, stumbling over Peggy in the hall. "I'm sorry," he mumbled.

There is so much to be sorry for, I thought. It was hard for me to close my eyes and go back to sleep. I fought sleep, fearful of dreaming, but I finally snuggled up to Peggy, and, feeling her closeness, closed my eyes.

Tuesday passed the same way as Monday. Peggy and I sat in the hall, watching people pass by and waiting for Daddy. At lunch time we got into the single file line and carried our plates out into the dining room. It seemed funny. Four days ago we hadn't been allowed to even go near the old BOQ. Now we were living in the new one. It was not like what we'd imagined. We were at war, and everything was different.

Tuesday became Wednesday. The flames on the *Arizona* were dying out. We sat, we slept, we awakened, we ate, we waited for Daddy.

Then a man I didn't recognize came into the cafeteria, his uniform wrinkled, his face old and tired. He headed for me and picked me up with his bandaged hand. I felt the stubble of sharp hairs on his cheek. It was Daddy; he had come.

I will never forget that moment, his hug, his smile, his voice.

"Dolph," Mother said, "I tried to make it to the shelter. I couldn't. I prayed for the girls, afraid they would get maimed by the gunfire. I asked God to take us, rather than maim Peggy and Joan."

"Alice, you did well. They're alright. You did well."

"I don't know who the Marine was that rescued us from the BOQ. At first he thought I'd spent the night there, sleeping with the men, and said he was ashamed of me. Then he saw the girls and apologized. He saved us. Can you find out who he was?"

Daddy's face softened. "I'll try to find him," he said. "I want to thank him, commend him." Daddy never found the Marine, though: the man must have been too embarrassed by his initial comments in the BOQ kitchen to identify himself.

"You can go home now. The *Arizona's* fire is out," Daddy continued. "The danger is past."

We were driven home, home toward the skeleton of the *Arizona*. We walked through the laundry room entrance, having been gone for three days. We could smell the rotting pork roast, still on the kitchen table, before we saw it. The onions were on the chopping board, now wilted and yellow. The sun shone through the windows, but I did not feel warm. I did not want to look out the front windows. The *West Virginia* was resting, sunk at her quay. I did not want to go out the front door. I did not want to walk down the bank to the water.

There were no bells, no ship's whistles. There were only the sounds of jackhammers.

The jackhammers pounded day and night as men tried to pierce the hull of the *Oklahoma* and rescue the sailors who were trapped inside, their faint rapping continuing to be heard. Once in awhile we would learn that another few had been saved. The jackhammers were to continue for several weeks. Peggy and I did not want the pounding sounds to stop: we wanted them to find the imprisoned men.

The butterfly, whose chrysalis we'd watched in our bedroom, was another casualty of war. He'd emerged, but he had had no food. His beautiful green, purple and black wings were folded up next to his body. Peggy and I named him "Blitz," mindful of our own blitzkrieg. We placed him in a small white box, between layers of cotton, and buried him under the papaya tree in the back yard.

Just then, a truck pulled up in front of the quarters. Two Marines got out and took down the sign that said, "Quarters T, Major Adolph Zuber, U.S.M.C.," and threw it into the back of their truck. They came back later in the afternoon and sawed the post that had held the sign off at its base.

"Mother, why did they take the sign and post down?" I made myself ask. "It's been there a long time "

"The Japanese may come back," Mother explained. "It's important that they do not know who lives where. All the signs and posts are being removed."

I felt like I was being erased. Like we were all being erased. The Japanese would not know who we were, and that was good. But nobody would ever know that we had lived here. I went out the back door, carefully avoiding the sight of the ships. Taking a small knife, I walked to the banyan tree in front of the old BOQ. I carved a Z in the tree, a sign that we had been here.

Toward evening, a third truck came. Three sailors went into the backyard and started digging the huge piece of the *Arizona's* plating that had penetrated two feet deep into the ground.

"Daddy, they got it out!" we exclaimed. "What if the *Arizona* had blown up five minutes later, while we were on the path?"

"I don't want to think about that," he replied. "I left soon after you three. I had a choice of doors -- the dining room or the living room. Something told me to leave through the door off the laundry room. A few moments later when the explosion came, I was knocked flat to the ground. We have much to be thankful for."

Except for the sound of the jackhammers, it was quiet in the quarters. Daddy was listening to Tokyo Rose on the shortwave radio. She was cajoling the men in the Philippines to give up, put down their weapons, and surrender. "Your fleet is destroyed. Nobody cares about you. There is no one to help you."

I hated her voice and her message. But the radio was our only link with the outside world. I wanted to scream, "We care! We may not be able to help, but we care." And then we found how much Janice Pritchard and Aunt Peggy cared about us.

Daddy came home and announced that the Red Cross had inquired to find out if our family was alive. "Alice, your Aunt Peggy sent them a top priority request that they find us and report back how we are. She told them that our quarters were on Battleship Row."

"Oh," sighed Mother. "How did she find that out? I never told her exactly where we lived, and I hoped she would think that we hadn't been in real danger."

"Well, it seems that she was so upset when she heard of the attack that she had to talk to someone. She went to her neighbor's house in Washington D.C., people she didn't even know. The little girl in the house was crying because her friends were dead. 'Joan and Peggy Ann are dead,' she kept saying."

"'Joan and Peggy Zuber?'

"'Yes.'"

By extraordinary coincidence, that little girl was Janice Pritchard. She had played with us on Ford Island, so she knew exactly where Quarters T was located. Aunt Peggy had listened to her, gone home, and called the Red Cross.

We all looked at Daddy. We hadn't thought about Janice. It was as though we were now cut off from the world. I remembered that Peggy and I used to wonder how big the headlines would be when we were bombed. We hadn't seen any newspapers on Ford Island. It would be many years before saw the size of the headlines for December seventh, the day that more than two thousand American servicemen died at Pearl Harbor.

"Life is certainly strange," Mother said quietly, "that Aunt Peggy would find out from Janice Pritchard on the other side of the world."

Mother had been sitting at her desk reading and then writing something. When she left the room, I read her message. It was written in red pencil on a U.S. Naval Air Station Coronado Commissary store sales slip, and it was titled "Flanders Field Today." A few of its words go as follows:

> . . . Quench the flowing lamp of hate
> Destroy its blood red wick . . .

> . . . The crosses their memory keep
> Poppies between them arranged. . .

Recent lines, written in pencil on yellow lined paper, now added:

> . . . And now add crosses for us here
> Hibiscus between them place
> Our peace has been erased.

Mother had written the opening of the poem one and one-half years ago in Coronado. She'd now completed it.

Days passed to the sounds of the jackhammers and Tokyo Rose, the voice of Japanese propaganda. Peggy and I haunted our Quarters T. We saw nobody. We were zombies. A week later, Daddy announced that the war against Japan meant we could no longer stay on the island. "It's too dangerous. You three must go into Honolulu and stay with the Davidsons."

Mother agreed reluctantly. She didn't want to leave Daddy. But the checkerboard ferry was now back in operation, and we would be able to take the green Pontiac off Ford Island.

How did I feel? I was past all feeling. I still had the sense of touch. I could feel cold and warmth, but I had quiescence of the heart. I was operating on automatic pilot. I did what I was told to do, went where I was told to go, and talked as little as possible.

Nine

The drive into Honolulu was harrowing. We went at night, and they kept stopping Mother at checkpoints. We were not allowed to show any light. The headlights of the Pontiac had been painted over with dark blue paint. Men with flashlights signaled us to slowly drive on through the dark night.

Peggy and I had a place to live in Honolulu at the Davidsons' house with the Colonel, his wife, and Sally and her little brother and the Japanese maid. That was all. Mother went back to Ford Island; she wanted to be with Daddy. I realize now that she knew how short her time was to be with him, that their future was indefinite. I had no thought of the future, only the now.

At the Davidsons' we were under complete blackout procedures at night. Air raid wardens patrolled the streets to detect any lights. One night someone at the Davidsons' left an interior light shining while opening a door.

A warden immediately rang the bell. "Put it out or I'll shoot it out," he threatened.

"Who let the light show?" Mrs. Davidson demanded.

It must have been one of the Davidson kids. Peggy and I were quiet. We had not lit a light at night since the attack.

The Davidsons had difficulty understanding our behavior. As a matter of fact, we hardly spoke. Mealtimes were a struggle.

"May I have the potatoes, please?" I asked at the dinner table.

"What's wrong with your manners?" Mrs. Davidson demanded. "It's 'Please may I have the potatoes?' 'Please' comes first."

What difference did it make? I wondered. What difference does it make whether "please" comes first or last? Please come to us, Mother, please. We need you.

On occasion, Mother did come to Honolulu and take us for a short drive. "Look!" she exclaimed on one such trip, "there are ships in the harbor!" It was December twenty-first and there were many new ships in the harbor: many sizes, all gray.

"Those ships have come in a convoy," she added.

What is a convoy? I wondered. Why was it waiting in the harbor? But she seemed distracted, saying, "The days are short. Time is short. I need to be with your father." My questions went unasked and unanswered.

There were no Christmas trees in Hawaii. The Matson ship bringing them over had run aground off the Oregon coast. So we cut off a branch of the algarroba tree growing in the Davidsons' back yard and decorated it.

I was no longer afraid I would die if pierced by one of the needles of an algarroba tree. That was good, because in one of their many arguments the Davidsons knocked the decorated branch, with all its barbed points, over onto Peggy. The spears hurt her; I could tell by the way she clenched her jaw. It was a tree, however: we decorated it and sat before it in our sunsuits.

Christmas morning came, and Peggy and I were waiting for Mother. She had called Christmas Eve to say that she was spending the night on Ford Island with Daddy and would come early in the morning. It was a strange Christmas morning: there weren't any presents. Colonel and Mrs. Davidson and Sally and the boys left us alone at ten o'clock to go visit friends. Peggy and I sat before the tree. Daddy had always loved to sing "O Tannenbaum" in German. I missed him. I missed our house. "O Christmas tree, O algarroba tree," I thought, "your needles are less sharp than my pain. . ."

The phone rang. I answered. It was a strange voice asking for the Davidsons. "They're out," I replied.

The voice continued, "As soon as they return have them call this number." I wrote down the number; we continued waiting.

Colonel Davidson read the message and called the number right after his return. He listened, hung up, turned, and said quickly to us, "Get your things. You're leaving on the convoy."

We hurried; there wasn't much to pack. But, we questioned, do we tell the Davidsons' Japanese maid? Do we say we are leaving? Yes, we tell her. She was our friend; she was not a spy. She wouldn't tell anyone a convoy was leaving. We hugged her goodbye, and in our sunsuits, with two small boxes, we were driven down to the harbor.

Peggy and Joan Zuber, seven and six

Opposing page: Aerial view of the Naval Operating Base, Pearl Harbor,
  looking southwest on 30 October, 1941
Top: Quarters T
Bottom: Admiral Bellinger's quarters

Top: Entrance to the "dungeon"
Right: View towards the harbor from a barred "cell" in the dungeon
Opposing: Navy family pass: American Red Cross card; Peggy's diary entry describing a blackout on March 23, 1941

Saturday   Mar 22 1941

2. Stayed in and cleaned
the house. Went to the
movies had fun

Sunday   Mar. 23, 1941

3. Went swim and at Mag, Daventons
Had good dinner, got a cut
from carl! Went to sleep two
times 20 min. Min. Got caught
on blackout, had to stay
on dock until boat came

*Opposing: Lei Day, May 1, 1941: Bay Bellinger, Mistress of Ceremonies; Peggy
    as Queen with her escorts; the Maypole
Major and Mrs. Adolph Zuber, Thanksgiving Dance, November, 1941*

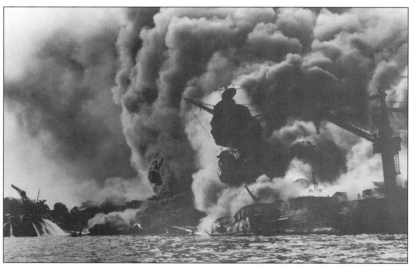

Top: Aerial view of Ford Island at beginning of attack. The white hospital ship SOLACE is in the upper left, just off the coastline adjacent to the Bellinger/ dungeo air raid shelter. Quarters T is just to the left of the column of white smoke. Bottom:USS ARIZONA burns furiously in front of Quarters T and the old BOQ

December 7, 1941: After the morning attack, the USS ARIZONA still burns.
The USS WEST VIRGINIA and the USS TENNESSEE after the Japanese attack on
Pearl Harbor.

Top: Japanese plane hit and burning; Bottom: A sky of fire: From the air rai
shelter, this was the view on the morning of the attack. Adjacent: Battleship
Row from the air a few days after the attack. Quarters T is in the middle of the
picture on the finger of land facing the ships' remains

Top: From Quarters T, the sounds of jackhammers operated by the men seen in the picture at left resounded day and night. Bottom: A Japanese plane wrecked during the attack

Top December 10, 1941. By this time, the family had returned to Quarters T on left side of picture just past the bow of the damaged USS TENNESSEE. Bottom: December 12, 1941. The Old BOQ is pictured between the masts of the damaged USS ARIZONA.

The convoy arrives in San Francisco December 31, 1941: Top: the Lurline, painted gray; Middle: Alice, Peggy, and Joan (carrying doll) after their interview for the Movietone news; Bottom: Injured sailor being carried off the Lurline

In San Francisco: Top: Joan gives her "V for Victory"
Bottom: Peggy and Joan on apartment roof in matching outfits their
*   mother had made*

Top: *Peggy Zuber Unger, Alice Brady Zuber, and Joan Zuber Earle at Quarters T in June of 1982*
Bottom: *Joan Earle (left rear) and two of her children (Robbie, left front and Alison, right front) with the Captain Barry Kunkel family, subsequent residents of Quarters T, in September of 1982*

Ten

We were ushered aboard a dark gray ship, funereal in color. What ship is this? I thought. And then I looked up and by the raised shape of the painted over letters I read the name I knew so well, L U R L I N E.

Mother was already aboard the ship. Right beside her on the deck were her typewriter and the boxes from Daddy's workshop. I recognized the one with my name and the one that said, "Peggy Ann," the boxes that Mother had packed last fall when she'd said she'd wanted to be ready. We had some clothes.

We were taken down to our cabin on D deck, in the bowels of the ship. Three walls of the room were lined with triple layer bunks, nine bunks in the room. But where were all the other passengers?

"Are the girls hungry? " a man asked.

"Yes," answered Peggy, "we've had nothing to eat since breakfast."

He guided us down to the dining room, down the wide staircase. I remember how it had looked when we sailed in 1940: men in tuxedos, women in long gowns. Peggy and I were now dressed in cotton sun suits; our uncombed hair hung in strands down our backs.

And then those forgotten words of a year ago greeted us, "It's the little English girls! The girls have survived!" We stood on the steps, hearing their voices; we could not believe that they remembered us. The waiters and waitresses of peacetime were still there, helping on the convoy.

Over the next two hours the *Lurline* began to receive her passengers: women, children and the wounded. Bodies on stretchers were gently brought up the gangplank and taken below deck. Peggy and I watched, waiting again for Daddy. Would he be able to come and say goodbye?

Yes! There he was, climbing up the gangplank, striding across the deck, putting his arm around Mother, talking to her softly, and then hugging us. Our goodbyes were hurried. The ship swelled with people, the wounded and evacuees, three times the normal complement of passengers, until there was no more room.

And then slowly, sorrowfully, the *Lurline* left the dock. There were no streamers to throw to friends on shore. There were no *leis*, no parting songs. I knew we might never come back. There is a legend that if you drop a *lei* off the ship and it floats back to the islands, you will return. We were not allowed to throw a scrap of paper off the ship. A submarine might find it and sink us.

I stood on the deck watching the horizon, wanting to see the islands as long as I could. They disappeared slowly. A loudspeaker interrupted my thoughts, "Attention! Everyone, attention! Wear your life jackets at all times!"

There were rules. Always wear your life jacket. Know your life boat location. Practice drills. Walk, don't run, to the your life boat. The loudspeaker blasted out orders; we obeyed. There was an ever-present fear that we might be torpedoed.

Four gray ships were in the center of the convoy. Destroyers bobbed up and down in the ocean surrounding the ships; a safety net in the water. We went down to our cabin to examine our bunks. There were no mattresses, just pieces of canvas, held in place by ropes. We were on D Deck, a death trap waiting for a torpedo. Our deck was so far below the main deck that if the ship turned over we would never get out. We decided to spend as much time as possible on the upper decks.

Peggy was seasick again, and there were no gumdrops to settle her stomach. She couldn't sleep or eat. I roamed the decks without her. The smell was horrible. There wasn't enough water; you weren't allowed to take a shower. Peggy was not alone in her seasickness: almost everyone seemed ill. Blackout curtains made of heavy dark cloth were placed at all entrances to the open decks. I had to be especially careful when I pushed aside the material, or I would step into a pile of vomit. I wanted to keep my shoes clean, because there was going to be a party on board. But I didn't want to go barefoot either.

I didn't get to go to the Christmas party the Red Cross held anyway; Mother wouldn't let me go. Only children under the age of ten could attend. "No," she said. "You're going to be ten in three days. You should let the younger children go."

I watched the children coming back from the party, presents in their hands. One girl clutched a toy train, something I'd always wanted. Sunk in my despair, I wished I could have shared in her happiness.

Days passed. I trailed like a shadow on the ship. Peggy spent most of her time on deck, the only place she felt less ill, wrapped up in blankets, telling stories to younger children. I listened to the grownups.

"There have been five babies born on the ship," I overheard a man say. I wondered how they looked and where they were.

We ate in three shifts, the people who could eat. I walked the ship looking silently at the sea. Where were we going? No one seemed to know.

December 29th came, and I was ten.

"Joan is ten today," Mother told the lady and her children at our table as we waited to be served in the dining room. She was trying to make me happy, but right then our dinner was interrupted when the loudspeaker blared, "Darken ship."

But that night, to me it didn't sound like "Darken ship," but more like "Abandon ship!" Everyone jumped up from their seats and began moving towards the door. Follow orders, I thought, starting off without my life jacket. Mother ordered me back, telling me not to panic.

Order returned. Mother and Peggy sang "Happy Birthday" to me. And then Peggy threw up.

The regular five-day trip took seven days as the convoy zigzagged across the ocean to avoid becoming a submarine's target. Rumors abounded as to where we would land: Seattle, San Francisco, Long Beach.

Peggy and I were going below decks to see Mother when the cry finally came, "Land!"

We ran back up the stairs and pushed aside the blackout curtain, forgetting the smells and the danger of stepping in vomit. We looked. There in the distance was the bridge, rust orange in color. At last we knew where we were. The *Lurline* plied resolutely through the water, slipping under the bridge, entering the bay. Everyone was cheering. We were home.

"Girls," Mother commanded, "we must go down below and freshen up." She stopped in the dining room and asked the steward for a soup bowl full of water. She then carried the bowl with its precious cargo carefully down to our cabin and washed our faces. She gently worked the snarls out of our hair and brushed back the curls. Out of one box came the navy blue suspender skirts, capes, and white blouses; out of another, our matching Panama hats.

"It's important to look your best," she commented while adjusting our hats in her final inspection. We walked up the stairs to the deck and sat on a bench. The ship docked, and the gangplank was lowered.

Doctors and nurses filed aboard, going to care for the wounded. Newsmen followed, standing on the deck, surveying the scene. Their eyes rested on the three of us.

"I want to take your pictures," said one man, overcoated against the cold air. "Please walk down the gangplank while we film you, and then give us an interview."

Peggy, Mother, and I did as he requested. Our feet touched the mainland -- safety -- while the man with the Movietone camera took our pictures. Then he listened to Mother's comments, after which he told us: "You'll be in the Movietone newsreels representing the 'Refugees from Pearl Harbor.'"

I wanted to correct him: we were not refugees, we were evacuees.

The camera whirled on. Peggy and I looked good on the outside, dressed up, our hair curled. But I did not feel good inside. We looked like the little English girls again, but we were really Marines now. We'd seen war. Someone stuck a doll in my arms to hold, but I had no interest in a doll. I was trying so hard to hold myself together.

The cameras eventually stopped. We were ordered back onto the ship where we stood for hours waiting to get off. Z's are always the last in line. This time we, the

Zuber family, were second to last; the Zumwalt family was behind us. Anyone seeing Movietone news would think that at least it was easy to disembark. But we waited our turn. Finally, finally, we walked down the gangplank and into the arms of the American Red Cross.

Eleven

1942

The cold San Francisco air whipped around us as we stood in line at the Red Cross information desk near where we'd docked. Mother answered the questions posed by the Navy Relief lady. Yes, we had some warm clothes. No, we had no place to stay. Mother seemed uncertain about where to go or what to do. No, we did not want travel arrangements made. Nobody was expecting word from us since impending arrivals of convoys were not being broadcast. Any announcement might alert Japanese submarines. We hadn't thought past our arrival. We had simply landed and now we needed a room for the night.

The Red Cross called and secured a room for us at the Stewart Hotel in downtown San Francisco. They would try to procure an apartment if we decided to stay. "Do you need a ride to the hotel?" they asked.

"No," replied Mother, "we can take a cab." She didn't want to disturb anybody, or have anyone take care of something she thought she could do herself. But, in retrospect, I see that she seemed like a somnambulist. She had accomplished her goal of getting us safely home, but the effort had depleted her already-slender emotional reserves.

The cab ride to the hotel was short: up Market Street, turning right at Geary. The driver said nothing, and we were silent. He didn't know that we had just arrived.

He carried our cardboard boxes and Mother's now somewhat battered typewriter case into the lobby. Our room was on the fifth floor and it had beds, real beds. Peggy took the small one, and I was to share the larger one with Mother. Better even than the beds, there was a bathroom with a tub and lots of hot water. We luxuriated in the tub; the seven days of washing ourselves in soup bowls filled with water were soon forgotten.

It was New Year's Eve, but there was nothing to celebrate. We were separated from Daddy and all that we had loved. We said little, ate our dinner in the room, and went to bed.

I poked Mother with my foot in the morning to wake her up. She ordered breakfast to the room, and rushed out to buy newspapers.

"Manila Fights On, But Hope Is Fast Fading: Greatest Russ Victory!" read the headlines of the *San Francisco Chronicle*. We sat in bed and read the papers. MacArthur was falling back in the Philippines. Hitler asked God to "Rescue Germany." Churchill was sure of Singapore. And the *Chronicle* announced that "There is More to Man Than the Eye Can See..." We read the papers. One column ended with:

> On this New Year's morning of 1942, it was the many moments when you stopped suddenly in the midst of your horn tooting and back-slapping to wonder, in sober sincerity about the future, and to pray fervently, deep down inside that this will be necessarily a victorious New Year. For victory will alone bring happiness.

I read and I thought in the Stewart Hotel. We were cut off from Daddy and we were cold.

We looked out the window of our room and saw snowflakes falling: the sky was weeping tiny frozen tears. I remembered the "liquid sunshine" in Hawaii that had caressed us and dried quickly on our skin. I remembered Pele, the Goddess of the Fire. Many had now been sacrificed in another fire. I did not think that Pele was happy.

Mother rushed out on Thursday and bought more papers. The weather was still cold. The paper said, "New Year Arrives in Red Flannels." Snow had fallen in San Francisco the night before, the first recorded snowfall since 1932. It had been 39 degrees outside on Wednesday, and the weatherman said the cold would continue.

"I'll have to get you girls some warm stockings, " said Mother.

"Warm stockings? What do you mean?" I asked.

"Heavy warm socks that you can pull over your knees. They will keep you warm," Mother tried to explain. I did not understand these warm stockings. Peggy and I were dark from the sun. We did not remember what cold was. We were going to find out.

Friday's newspapers told our story. The *San Francisco Call-Bulletin* reported:

> From San Francisco, fanning out in every direction west, streams of evacuated Honolulu residents were *en route* to their mainland homes and relatives today in trains, private cars and chartered buses.

And the *Chronicle* said:

> From hotels, private homes and public buildings, since they arrived Wednesday . . . scores were on their way home.

"Home? Where is home? We're still here," I wanted to say. We had a hotel room, but where would we go from here?

Mother cut out the stories from the newspapers and put them in an envelope, "I am saving these," she said. "Someday you may want to read them." I didn't think about someday. I was thinking about now. And then the hotel phone rang, and someone on the other end told Mother that an apartment had been found.

"We're very lucky," Mother said, "I have found us a furnished apartment."

I didn't feel lucky. I didn't feel anything. Peggy didn't either; she told me so. Mother was, if just barely, still in command. She fell apart at night and came back together, if a little more slowly, each morning.

We walked to the apartment. It was on Jones Street, right up from its corner intersection with Post. Jones Street looked like a wall of apartment buildings, punctuated by entries, marching up the street.

"It'll be fun. You can ride the cable cars just like you did when we lived on Goat Island!" Mother exclaimed. It didn't look like fun. Early that first week she bought us Navy blue knee-high socks. Our legs were warm after that, but we were still cold.

In order to get into the building, we had to press a button. A bell rang, which Mother explained opened the door and allowed us to enter. Then we got into an elevator that made rickety sounds and strange moans as it crawled all the way up to the sixth floor.

The hall smelled of a thousand different odors mixed into one overwhelming odor of what someone was cooking for dinner. Gone were the scent of flowers and warm embracing air; the cold air hugged my body.

We opened the front door of the apartment. There was a small entry room with a twin bed; this would be

100

Peggy's bed. There was one room with windows facing a brick wall of the building next door. Big wooden panels graced one wall. Mother demonstrated how the panels opened to expose the wall bed behind. I looked at the bed I would have to share with Mother.

There were two other small rooms in the apartment: a bathroom off the entry hall, and a tiny kitchen off the living room-bedroom. There was a small window in the kitchen and, by straining our necks and looking straight up, we could see the sky. We could hear the cable cars rumbling up the street. I didn't say anything; I took in what I saw and tried to figure out what I thought.

"Mother, this sofa is scratchy," I announced as I sat on the harsh fabric of the green sofa. So is the other chair." I didn't like to complain, but when I put my face on the side of the chair it hurt.

"They are frieze fabric chairs. Frieze lasts longer," Mother explained. I decided that frieze chairs lasted longer because nobody wanted to sit in them, but I didn't want to say anything more. Instead, I mentally counted the ways out of the apartment. There were only two: the front door and the fire escape visible through the main room's windows.

There was nothing familiar in the apartment: no rose blossom-covered rattan sofa, no books, no toys, no globe, no china, nothing at all. Everything we owned outside of the boxes and Mother's typewriter was back in Quarters T. I felt empty, hollowed out.

Our first trip out was to the pharmacy on the corner across the street. "We need necessities," Mother said. She led and we followed, picking out what we needed: soap, toothpaste, toothbrushes, Kleenex, and toilet paper. The clerk at the cash register started talking to Mother.

"I was at my brother's home in Daly City when they announced the attack," the lady said. "We couldn't believe it at first!"

"We were there, in Pearl Harbor," Mother answered.

The lady did not seem to understand. She kept talking about where she was when she heard, "The attack was a complete surprise. I was out in the yard when they called me in to listen."

I wanted to say, "No, it wasn't a surprise. We were ready. We knew it was coming." I wanted to speak, but I couldn't.

Nobody listens, I thought. I couldn't speak. I could look and think, but I couldn't talk. There was no way to describe where we had been or what we had seen. This silence was to continue for both Peggy and me; we bottled up our feelings and memories. We needed to talk, but there was nobody to listen.

"They're showing movies of the attack at the news theaters on Market Street," Mother announced.

Bundled up against the cold, we walked down to Market Street where there were two theaters showing almost the same scenes. We went first to one, then the other. I watched in horror. One of the films had the sound track dubbed in, starting out with the ships that had been attacked while in dry-dock. This was the only part of the attack that we had not witnessed. Then the film showed different views of the burning *Arizona*. One sequence captured the old BOQ that we had been in when the *Arizona* exploded.

And then I looked and exclaimed, "There is Quarters T, right beyond the *Arizona's* broken mast! I can see our front door!"

The other film started off differently, with pictures of the Hickam Field entrance. Then it switched to the *Arizona* and, for a split second, I saw our quarters again.

People were sitting around us in the theater, talking, pointing at the ruins.

Suddenly, I wanted to leave. It was too sad, I could not bear to watch it any longer. I could feel my body tightening up. I did not have to see pictures to remember; I could close my eyes and see it all again. I would always remember.

"Mother, I have to go. This brings it all back," I said. Rising quickly, I left the theater.

Peggy followed. We never did see the Movietone newsreel of our arrival in San Francisco, but Daddy later told us he'd seen it while he was at Pearl Harbor.

The next weekend, Mother took us out to visit a friend in a part of San Francisco where there were houses. Her friend talked. "Well, it wasn't a surprise to us. We knew it was coming, and we started to get ready." Her words sounded like boasts, telling us how smart she was, and then she led us down to her basement.

There were rows and rows of shelves in her basement holding cans of food, bags of sugar and flour, tins of shortening and coffee. The room looked like a store. I wanted to scream at her, "You are a hoarder!" I knew what hoarders were: people who took more than they needed.

I did not say anything to Peggy or Mother. That would have been "impolite." But I thought of the boxes we had landed with and the bare furnished apartment with no reminders of our former life. The windows that looked out on a wall and a fire escape. I could not understand this lady's greed, nor the insensitivity of the clerk at the store. We were there, I wanted to say, while you were hoarding. But I could not speak. I was a silent passenger in a strange world that did not listen or understand.

And yet Peggy and I not only had to pretend that everything was all right, but also to start in a new school.

Mother registered us at Redding School on Pine Street. First we had to walk up Jones, turn on Pine and walk four blocks toward Van Ness. Redding School is still there, and children still attend it, but even in 1942 it wore the mantle of urban blight. A three-story brick building, it was shaped like a huge U. In the open U between two wings was a tiny asphalt playground. Another playground was built on the roof. There were no trees. There was no grass or flowers. There was nothing to do on the playground because it was so small that everybody ran into each other. No one said, "Please," or "Thank you" or "Excuse me." Nobody cared if someone else fell down.

We waited in lines on the playground for the signal to enter the wide echoing halls and the marble steps that led to the upper floors. I ran my hand over the worn wood banisters as I climbed the stairs. Gone was the gentle laughter, the rest hour on *lauhala* mats on the *lanai*, the songs. Gone, gone, gone.

The class was way behind Kenneth Whiting School. These were urban kids. They had not even begun fractions. We had finished them in Hawaii and had gone on to decimals and percents. My teacher was old and had grizzled gray hair and a limp. The children said that a large spool of butcher paper had accidentally rolled over her leg at school, and that that was the reason why she limped and why they kept her at the school.

I tried to tell Mother that the work was too easy, but it was very hard to talk to her and she didn't seem to care. She did not visit the school again once she had registered us. Pretty soon we lost our key, and sometimes when we came home in the afternoon Mother was now asleep and didn't hear the buzzer. When that happened, Peggy and I now had to use the other entrance into the apartment: we'd take turns climbing up the six sets of metal stairs on the fire escape and through our window. Then we'd press the buzzer and let the other enter the building.

The children in Redding School knew we were different. We looked innocent, and they had no way of knowing how we'd aged. We did not speak their language. We were set off, out of place. Some children accused us of being "shell-shocked," a term we resisted.

In one way, we were very naïve. "What's cooking, good looking?" one boy yelled at us as we walked home. Another girl said something sexy back to him. I was shocked by her boldness. But when I tried to tell Mother about it, she was busy typing and didn't want to be interrupted.

Our worst angst came when the air raid sirens went off at school. We two knew the siren meant a common danger that all had met together on Ford Island. When the air raid drills were sounded at Redding School, the children were instructed to leave immediately and run home. No one was to loiter. That meant that Peggy and I could not run together. There were horrible minutes when we didn't know if the other one was safe.

Mother had a charge account at the grocery story around the corner on Post. Peggy and I would buy lots of candy and cookies. Sometimes Peggy would cook. We came home, read, ate, slept, and went back to school. In many ways, we took care of ourselves.

Twelve

Sometimes Peggy and I would go down alone to the Chinese Restaurant on the Northwest corner of Post and Jones and charge our dinner. There was a bar in front; we would sit at a table in back and talk softly to each other, remembering our dinners at the Ford Island Officer's Club and the bowls of chocolate syrup without ice cream.

One evening Peggy looked up and said, "Look, there are two Marines coming in!"

We looked at them; they looked at us and smiled, and then one said, "Why, you're Major Zuber's daughters! You look the same. You haven't changed!"

Peggy and I were ecstatic. They knew us; they understood us! We sat and talked about Daddy and Hawaii.

But Mother wasn't happy when we ran home to tell her our news. "You girls know that you must never talk to strangers. You cannot eat there again."

I looked at her, listened, and swallowed my voice.

Daddy wrote us letters. We watched the mail box slot each day, hoping for news. His Marines had packed up everything in Quarters T, but he did not know when the shipment would reach the mainland or when or where the faithful green Pontiac would be delivered.

107

> I have received your report cards from
> Kenneth Whiting School and will be
> forwarding them on to you. I will not be able
> to send any greeting cards. They are not
> considered acceptable mail. From now on we
> must use only plain white paper and white
> envelopes. These are censorship rules and if
> they are not followed, letters will not be
> passed on.

Each word in his letters meant something to us, and we looked daily for his plain white envelopes.

One afternoon, Mother dressed us once more in our navy blue skirts, capes, and Panama hats. "We must send pictures to your father." Peggy's skirt was now so short that it came above her knees. I didn't think that she'd ever be able to wear it again. The first pictures were taken in the entrance to the apartment building. I held up my fingers in a "V for Victory" signal.

"Smile, Joan, smile for Daddy," Mother admonished. The corners of my mouth turned up. The rest of the pictures were taken on the tar and asphalt roof of the building. We took turns snapping the pictures. Mother looked nice that day, wearing a hat with a big bird on the top. She wanted us to look happy.

She studied my face and teased me gently. "Joan, what has happened to your smile? I don't see it anymore."

I didn't know where my smile had gone. I really couldn't think of anything to smile about.

We were on the roof, and, for me, the roof and the basement were the two most important spots in the building. I spent most of my time in these two places.

I made a deal with Mother that I would do the laundry: five cents for each sheet and two cents apiece for each piece I washed. I would bundle up all the clothes, take them to the elevator, press "B" for basement, and descend into the bowels of the building. I started up the old wringer washing machine there, turning on the water hose, putting in the soap and the laundry, and waited as it went through the wash cycle. I then drained the water, waited through the rinsing, and finally, slowly and carefully, fed the material through the two white rubber rolling bars of the wringer.

The wet clothes were heavy, but I picked the baskets up, pressed "R" for roof on the elevator panel, and went to the roof to hang it all up on the coarse white clothesline. I remembered the clothesline on the grass behind Quarters T, in the shade of the papaya trees, where clothes would dry quickly in the warm air.

Peggy and I often met on the gray ugly roof. "Let's make a sandbox," she suggested. "We can ride the street car out to the beach, fill up bags of sand, and make a pile here."

I looked at the roof and calculated how many bags of sand we'd have to carry to make a big enough pile to play in. I knew we couldn't carry enough. There would be no sand or grass in our lives.

But there was one wonderful thing we could do on the roof. We could stand looking towards the harbor and watch the convoys come in. When we saw the first one, we were so excited.

"Do you think Daddy is on this one?" Peggy asked me.

"I hope so," I answered, saying an inner prayer. It wasn't answered, but Peggy and I made a pledge: we would come up to the roof every day and watch for the ships.

We waited for Daddy to come, and, while we waited, others left. There was a Japanese American student in my class. The other children talked about her. I wondered why. I didn't care that she was Japanese; she was not the enemy. She was an American just like me, and her face mirrored my sadness. One day she was absent from the classroom, and the teacher said that she was not coming back. The students talked about her some more, their words circling about my head. I said nothing. I had accepted the disappearance of things and people. I did not worry about spies or another air raid. I had had mine.

We no longer ran home from school when the air raid siren sounded during the day. They had changed the auditorium of Redding School into a bomb shelter. Additional cement was poured along the outer wall and sandbags were piled against it for additional protection. We practiced the drills weekly, following instructions, "When the planes come, you will march down to the auditorium quietly, no running, no talking." the principal announced.

We also had blackouts at night; we pulled heavy blackout shades down on the three apartment windows to seal in the light.

The other children were scared, and the school attempted to keep up their morale. Each morning before school, the custodian would unlock the auditorium, and students would perform on the stage. Many fathers were at war, and mothers were working in the shipyards. These mothers left their apartments early, dropping their children off at school. We all met in the auditorium. Peggy and I would go up on the stage and do the hula and sing the old songs of Hawaii. The audience clapped a little, but they didn't sing "Aloha Oe" along with us. I would close my eyes and hear the music as I swayed, and for a few minutes, I'd forget the cold mornings as I moved my bare feet on the warm wooden stage. I'd remember again the feel of grass, the kiss of the air, and the scent of flowers.

After school Peggy and I collected tin cans for the war effort, becoming the official tin can collectors for the apartment building. We talked to people as we collected, and then we took the cans to our apartment, removed the labels, washed them out, and removed the other lid. The best part was flattening them. I pretended I was stomping on the enemy as I squashed the cans with my foot. Some of the cans were messy, but we didn't care.

We collected tin foil as well. First we would collect all the foil from Mother's cigarette packages and our gum wrappers, then we would empty the collection box we'd set up in the lobby of the building. We separated the tin foil from the wrappers and pressed it into a ball which became larger and heavier each week. Then we'd deliver the cans and the foil balls to the war effort. We were doing what our father would want us to do: we were doing our part.

Thirteen

1942 - 1943

Easter Morning, April 13, 1942, found us standing with thousands of other San Franciscans watching a parade go down Market Street. It was pouring rain, not our soft "liquid sunshine," but cold dampening rain. We were wearing our new yellow rain slickers, and I felt proud.

We looked at the newspaper the next day, April 14, where a big picture of the Easter Parade on the front page of the *San Francisco Chronicle* showed the marching men and the crowds along the sidewalk. Two children in rain slickers stood on the curb in front of the crowd. We cut out the picture and put it in the box with Mother's other clippings.

And then our furniture arrived from Hawaii. We went down and looked at the crates in the warehouse. Every box was unmarked, so Mother didn't know where anything was. She wanted to find her sewing machine, but she gave up looking after the workers opened up two crates and still couldn't find it. But they did find the table silver in the basket of our washing machine. I wondered in which crate Ferdinand the Bull was, and if his cork tree was near him. I felt he must have missed his flowers the way I missed mine.

After a month-long search, we did find the Pontiac and bring it home and put it in the garage.

Peggy came into the apartment one day, and I saw that she was trembling as she dropped the groceries she had bought on the couch. Mother had told us to be careful about opening the foyer door into the apartment house. "Don't open the door if anyone is around. They might follow you in." she'd warned. But she had not warned us about people on the street.

"I was walking up to the apartment when a man approached. He didn't look like a bum, but he was weaving. He passed me, and I thought I was safe. But then I heard his footsteps stop and come back towards me." Peggy rushed her words. "I hurried towards the foyer and took out my key to open the door, but he was too fast. I put my key back in my pocket, and then he tried to corner me on one side of the foyer. I set down the groceries and dodged him by going left. He was smiling with a crazy look, and his breath was horrible. I gave him a push and he fell backwards."

"How did you get away?" I asked.

"Louie, the garage man, came around the corner and chased him away. Joan, I was -- and I am -- frightened. What should I do?"

We talked together. Mother was asleep and could not help us. We decided never to go out at night alone. In the future we would always walk together.

And then we finally got some good news: we had to find a new apartment. Mother said that the present one was too small. She read the advertisements every day. We read them too: anything to get away from Jones Street and from Redding School.

She took us out in the Pontiac, driving down the San Francisco peninsula to look at one place that was like a farm. It was near a small town and had lots of grass.

"Girls, you'd have to do a lot of walking if we lived here," she said. "Gas is strictly rationed, going for military use."

But I didn't think Mother was worried about gas; she wanted to stay right in San Francisco because it felt closer to Daddy.

"We love to walk," we answered. "The air smells delicious."

But Mother turned it down. She said she was worried about gas and that the new school wouldn't be good. I realized that she did not know how bad Redding School was.

She no longer knew how we felt.

Peggy and I scoured the newspaper want ads looking for a new apartment and found one "near Grant School," which meant, we decided after we'd carefully consulted a map, that it was a long way from Redding School. We cajoled Mother into going to see it.

The apartment was light and airy, it was only on the second floor, and, best of all, it had three doors out.

We took Mother there twice, wanting her to see how nice it would be to live there. The place had grass and trees. Grant School, nearby, was only two stories high and was a cheerful stucco, but Mother said, "No, it is just too large."

Peggy and I looked at each other in dismay.

Mother did find a new apartment just around the corner on Post Street. It was on the fifth floor, which meant that we'd only have to climb five stories on the outside fire escape. Mother got us identification charms with "749 Post Street" engraved on them. We would have to stay at Redding School. There was no chance to escape; she'd signed a one-year lease.

The new apartment was larger. There was a living room where Mother could sleep, with a large bay window looking out at the other apartment houses. A door led into our bedroom, where Peggy and I shared a double bed; she would no longer be alone in a hall. The kitchen was larger, and there was more light.

The days became warmer, and Peggy and I started investigating San Francisco. The main branch of the library, a large and impressive granite building filled with books, was a short walk away. I began reading my way through the thousands of books, bringing them back and forth from the library in a large brown paper shopping bag. The bottom of the bag burst one time, spilling all the books in the middle of a busy intersection. I was embarrassed as I stooped to pick them up.

We were no longer reading *Nancy Drew* or *Adventure Girls* books; that ended in Hawaii. I didn't want to finish reading *Under the Lilacs*. Bab's and Betty's tea party ended for me on December seventh. They were not important to me any more.

On warm summer days, Peggy and I took the streetcar out to the Ocean Beach Boardwalk and rode the "Shoot the Chutes." A small car on a track would climb a steep hill and then rush downward like a roller coaster and dump us in the water. We didn't mind getting wet. The bumper cars came next, where we would try to crash or not to crash as we rode around the large ring. Then we would slide down the two-story wooden slides on pieces of cloth. I loved the feeling of plummeting down; it was like flying free.

We walked together up the street to the large building that contained the Sutro Baths. I was not impressed with the different pools. I wanted to swim outdoors like we had on Ford Island. The Fleishhshacker Pool in Golden Gate Park was so large that we were afraid to swim in it. Everything about San

Francisco was contrasts: the sun and the fog, the apartments and the houses, the cement school playground and the grass in the park.

"If you don't get out of the yard, I'll shoot you," yelled a man from the second story window of a huge house near the top of Nob Hill. He leaned out of the window and showed us his shotgun.

Peggy and I looked at each other and ran. We'd been playing in what we thought was a vacant lot, filled with tall weeds and anise plants. We loved the anise plants; we could break off a small branch and smell licorice. The lot had been our playground close to home, and we were sorry to lose it, but we didn't want to be shot at again. December seventh had been enough.

That left us with only one place to play close to home: the small Washington Park at the top of Nob Hill. We had to walk up Jones Street to reach it, first the steep hill and then the stairs of the steepest part.

Peggy said, "Pretend that there is a magical rope pulling us up."

I would concentrate and pretend really hard. It worked! The last block was the easiest to climb. We passed the Fairmont Hotel, crossed the street, and there was the park. It was tiny and had signs on the sloping grass that said, "Stay off the grass." There was no sand to play in. It was not a very happy place to visit.

The movie "Bambi" opened that year in San Francisco theaters. Long lines appeared in front of the Golden Gate Theater; everyone was going, and we were too. That is, until Mother got mad at us. I'm not really sure why she said we couldn't go: it continued to be difficult for us to know when we would be able to do something and to count on it.

But somehow we patched things back up with Mother and went to see the movie. It was beautiful but so sad. When Bambi's mother was shot, I felt her wound. Peggy and I had seen enough killing.

I knew that Mother was terribly sad. Sometimes I saw pieces of paper with half-written poems. The writing was scraggly and I could only read a few words. "Dolph," "need you," "without you." There were times when she seemed far away, and then suddenly she would start paying attention to us again.

She decided that I was too thin and took me to a doctor who suggested cod liver oil. But I didn't think tonic would help me gain weight. I missed the eggnogs she used to make with thick fluffy whites dotted with nutmeg on the top. I missed turkey dinners. I thought I could gain weight if only I could taste stuffing again.

September 1942 came, and back we went to Redding School, starting the sixth and seventh grades. I had a young teacher who seemed to like children. The first week of school, she gave us a list of all the math pages we would do during the year. By November, I had finished the list and was planning to read instead.

Peggy was not so lucky. Her teacher had a reputation for meanness, often shoving children and even occasionally knocking them down. From my classroom down the hall, I could hear her shrill teacher's voice.

Peggy also began to lose her smile. We still met on the roof of the new apartment and watched for convoys and for Daddy.

"Girls, you can pick out the largest Christmas tree you can carry," Mother announced to us. "It will make up for last year, and we can leave it up until your father comes home."

The tree was almost too large for the elevator. Peggy and I pushed it in and bent the top. We squeezed into the corners to avoid its leafy branches, half-pulling and half-carrying it through the apartment door and into the living room. We moved all the furniture aside and set the tree in front of the bay window making sure it would be the first thing besides us that Daddy would see when he arrived.

We decorated the tree with homemade ornaments; all the old, familiar ornaments were in some crate at the warehouse. Although we were older and really knew the truth, we were careful not to offend Santa Claus, remembering Mother's story about the book he kept at the North Pole with children's names. According to Mother, if you uttered your disbelief in him he would tear your page out of his book. Every time you felt a sharp breeze, she'd said, it was some disbelieving child's page dropping to the ground.

The days passed. Christmas vacation was over and we went back to school. The tree still stood in the middle of the living room, its needles getting brittle and dropping on the rug. Peggy and I insisted on leaving it up. It was our symbol of hope.

We had one celebration in the Spring of 1943: "This is the Army" by Irving Berlin came to the San Francisco War Memorial Opera House. Mother wrote us excuses from school and we sat in the huge room listening to the songs. "You're in the Army, Mr. Jones," and "Oh, How I Hate to Get Up in the Morning." But it was the part about the bugle in reveille that Peggy and I loved: "You gotta get up, you gotta get up, you gotta get up, It's morning." We knew what reveille sounded like. We remembered.

And then, suddenly, Peggy was sick. Really, really sick. Mother, caring for her, seemed temporarily better. She took Peggy to the doctor after two days of high fever. Peggy was given many blood tests; the tentative diagnosis was rheumatic fever. The doctor came by

119

daily to see her in the apartment; I sat on the bed and talked to her, lost in worry.

Peggy was in bed for three weeks. The doctor was worried about her heart and said that she must have absolute rest; she could not be disturbed about anything. When she was finally able to get up and walk around, Mother surprised us both by asking, "Would you like a dog, Peggy? A dog would keep you company."

Of course Peggy wanted a dog! So Bonnie, a little mixed breed toy collie with a long, skinny tail, entered our lives. During Peggy's convalescence, we walked the downtown streets of San Francisco to Union Square with Bonnie. We were happy together, the three of us.

But I was lonely during the day, going to school without Peggy. We had always walked together, and when she was well enough to go back I rejoiced. Mother called the school and told them that Peggy was to rest frequently, take it easy, and not get excited.

The first day she was back, after school I stood on the tiny playground waiting for her to come down. She was late. I waited more minutes. Where was she? I asked another student if she had seen my sister, and was told that the teacher was keeping her after. "The teacher knocked her down, and when Peggy didn't apologize, she told her to stay after."

I ran up the marble steps, entered her classroom, and saw Peggy, white faced and shaking, sitting at her desk crying. I was both scared and angry, and in my anger I suddenly found my voice.

I marched up to the teacher's desk and, looking her squarely in the eye, said, "You know that Peggy must not be upset."

The teacher ignored me.

Now I yelled, "My sister's been very ill. She's not to be excited in any way. And if she dies, it's going to be your fault!" The sound of my words echoed in my ears.

The teacher screamed at me, "Get out of this room and never come back!"

I ran out the door, almost colliding with the principal, who'd been alerted by all the shouting.

I went back down to the playground and waited. I scuffed my shoes on the asphalt and waited some more. Then I went back upstairs and found that they had taken Peggy into the teachers' restroom, where she was lying down. When Peggy was calm, the principal helped her down the stairs and we walked home together.

We were sisters, wrapped in each other, waiting for Peggy to recover, walking Bonnie together, and waiting for Daddy to come home.

We had not seen him in a year and a half. During that time, we'd exchanged letters and we'd mailed him some shoes because his size, 13EEE, was almost impossible to find, but there'd been no visits and no phone calls.

As the days grew warmer and Peggy grew stronger, we enlisted the aid of Burt, a boy my age, and began to plant a Victory Garden in the rocky yard behind the apartment building. First we had to remove all the junk, and then Burt and I tried to shovel the hard soil. We planted carrots, beans, beets, and cabbage. We got very grimy. It was almost like playing in the sand, and, besides, we were helping the war effort. We watered, defying the older occupants in the building who felt that the shaded garden would never grow.

And then we watched as the tiny shoots thrust themselves through the ground.

We could look up at the apartment bay window and see the shadow of the now completely dead Christmas tree. It was time to take it down. There was no way we could bend the brittle branches of the tree to fit in the elevator, so instead we cut it up into pieces and dropped the trunk out the open bay window, praying that it would not land on our Victory Garden and damage the plants.

One cold Saturday morning in June of 1943, Peggy stepped on a piece of glass when she got out of bed and had to go to the clinic by herself for stitches: Mother called the Navy Hospital and a cab for Peggy. Mother was resting in her room.

I turned on the small electric heater by our bed to warm up the room. The glowing red coil entranced me. What would happen, I wondered, if I placed a piece of paper against the coils?

I found out. The paper caught on fire. Frightened, I dropped the burning piece into the trash can. Then the trashcan caught on fire. I panicked. What to do now? I picked up the can, ran to the window, opened it with a shove, and dropped the basket out, down five stories.

Mother came in, sniffing. "I smell smoke!"

"You do?" I answered. "There isn't any fire in here." But I was not clever enough to fool Mother. I confessed, and she galvanized into action, moving faster than I had seen her move since Pearl Harbor.

"Joan, you may have set the yard on fire!" Without waiting for my answer, she rushed to the elevator, down, and out into the yard. I could see her, far below, turning on the hose, watering the yard and the Victory Garden until she was satisfied that the fire was out.

Lunchtime came. Peggy returned in another cab, and Mother began worrying if we should sign the lease for another year on the apartment. The new lease had to be signed by the following Friday.

She'd been trying to find out when Daddy might return. We listened as she called a Marine officer friend of Daddy's in San Francisco. "Do you know when Dolph will be coming home?" she asked quietly.

She held the phone out for us to hear the man's answer: "He arrived in San Francisco half an hour ago. He's in my office now. Do you want to speak with him?"

Daddy spoke. He was close by! He would be at the apartment in an hour!

Peggy and I rushed down to wait at the entrance to the apartment house. We searched the street with our eyes. And then at last here he came, a tall proud Marine, our father.

He swept me up in his arms and hugged me. I felt the warmth of his body, the fabric of his uniform, the feeling of safety.

As he lowered me down, my arm caught on the anchor of his Marine insignia. It was a small puncture wound and it bled, and I was surprised to notice that it hurt. But on June 5, 1943, at 2:45 in the afternoon, I was relieved of active duty in the United States Marine Corps.

My tour of duty was over.

In Others' Words:
Accounts from Men in War

U. S. NAVAL AIR STATION
PEARL HARBOR, T. H.

10 December, 1941

INCIDENT OF ENTERPRISE AIRPLANES, ATTEMPT LANDING.
I was in the landplane control tower when the six Enterprise planes were fired upon. Lt. Comdr. Young, Commander of the Enterprise Air Group, was also present and assumed control to bring the planes in. Two flood light trucks with lights on were stationed at the southwest end of the runway and green lights were placed at the northwest end to mark the corner of the runway. The following is the traffic that passed between the tower and the planes:
TOWER: Turn on your running lights, make approach from Barbers Point. Come in as low as possible.
PLANE: (Believed to be Blue 18): Am making one pass at the field.
TOWER: Do not make pass at field. Turn on running lights and come in as low as possible.
BLUE 18: (To planes in formation): Close in. I am going to make one pass at the field. (The planes were then approx. over drydock channel.)
TOWER: Do not make pass at field, come straight in. (At this time firing started apparently from surface vessels.)
ONE OF THE PLANES: What in hell is wrong down there?
TOWER: Turn off lights and beat it. (One plane got on the field during the firing. Later instructions were again given to approach low from Barbers' Point with running lights on and come straight in. Only one other plane of this group managed to get it.

/s/ F. A. ERICKSON,
Lieut., U.S.C.G.

U.S. NAVAL AIR STATION
PEARL HARBOR, T. H.

10 December, 1941

MEMORANDUM:

From: Operations Officer
To: Commanding Officer
      During the early evening of December 7, 1941, I
received word that friendly planes were approaching to
land on Ford Island. Reliable men were sent out in
cars, motorcycles, etc. to warn all riflemen, machine
gun nests, etc. to hold fire. After several false
alarms as to the immediacy of the approach of these
planes, word came through which led me to believe the
planes would be landing in a very short time. I again
ordered the word passed to the defense forces, having
particular regard to men stationed adjacent to the
southwest portion of the field, from which direction
the planes would normally approach. I then drove to
the Luke Field side and took position well out on the
warming up platform at hangar #133 in order to direct
planes to their parking area and give what service
might be needed. After a few minutes I saw the planes
approaching from the direction of Hickam Field. At
first I saw only four planes in sections of two each.
An instant later I saw that one section had three
planes and heard one of the men with me say "There's
six of them." I never saw the sixth plane. All
running lights were burning brightly and the planes
appeared to be flying up the Pearl Harbor Channel. I
believe they must have been in the close vicinity of
Hospital Point when I heard the first shots fired. In
less than five seconds the entire Pearl Harbor area was
firing. The planes flew up drydock channel at an
estimated 300 feet altitude until they disappeared from
my view at a point a little northeast of the
administration building.
                              /s/ E.B. WILKINS,
                              Lt. Comdr., U.S.N.

MARINE BARRACKS
U.S. NAVAL AIR STATION
PEARL HARBOR, T.H.

16 December, 1941

REPORT OF ACTION OF MARINE BARRACKS DURING JAPANESE AIR
RAID OF DECEMBER 7, 1941

At about 7:55 a.m. on the morning of 7 December,
1941, I heard small arms fire outside my bedroom
window. I looked out the window and saw a plane
discharging a torpedo against the USS West Virginia.
The explosion followed almost immediately. By this time
the 5 inch battery of the West Virginia was in action.
I sent my family to the air raid shelter at Quarters K,
called up the Sergeant of the Guard to have all
automatic weapons sent to the roof of the barracks to
engage the enemy planes. While at the telephone, the
first attack by the low flying bomber was made by the
enemy. I looked out the window and saw a big blood red
fire on the USS *Arizona* which seemed to have its root
between turret no. 2 and the foremast. There were no
men on the bow and only a few on the stern. I felt that
the ship would blow up at any time so I ran out the
back door of my quarters. The explosion occurred when I
had taken about five steps from the rear door. I hailed
Admiral Bellinger, who was passing, and I was driven to
the Marine Barracks.

Upon my arrival at the barracks, the Marines were
already in action. I had all the ammunition broken out,
and sent to the Armory for additional automatic weapons
and ammunition. Men were set to cleaning additional
weapons and to belting additional ammunition.

Just about this time a bomb exploded squarely in
the center of the Station Dispensary. Thinking that
there would be a serious loss of life, I asked for
volunteers to carry all wounded men out of it.
Practically every able bodied man not engaged in firing
at the enemy responded and in short order all wounded
were transferred to the Marine Barracks and the mess

127

hall. Guards were stationed to direct all wounded men into the above places.

About 2:00 p.m. with the sanction of the Commissary Officer, Naval Air Station, I obtained 1500 cots and three field kitchens from the Navy yard. Billets were established and mess began immediately.

Marines worthy of especial commendation are:

Acting corporal James D. Young, with his color detail consisting of Privates Frank Dudovick and Paul O. Zeller who stood at attention awaiting the officer of the day's order to run up the colors even though they were strafed and bombs fell nearby.

Private Donald E. Bramlette who from his post at the officers quarters helped many survivors in the water to safety, despite the constant bombing and strafing of the enemy.

Sergeant Hubert L. Breneman who continuously during the enemy action, brought in from exposed points, to the sick bay, many disabled and badly wounded men.

Corporal Clifton Webster, who from an exposed position atop the crew's barracks, fired a large burst of Lewis machine gun fire into the cockpit of a low flying Japanese bomber, causing it to crash into the channel.

Especially commendable was the action of the crews of the small boats of the Naval Air Station. With utter disregard for their personal safety they continuously performed the duty of rescuing survivors from dangerous positions near the bombed ships.

I was particularly proud of the action of the Marines under my command. They executed every order with an amazing speed and with utter disregard of personal safety.

/s/ADOLPH ZUBER
Major, U.S. Marine Corps

Epilogue

Within a month of Daddy's arrival home, we were living again as a family -- now in San Diego, warmed by the temperate air, soothed by the swaying palm trees and the joy of being reunited. Blue flags with gold stars began to appear in many windows, acknowledging the ultimate sacrifice by a father, son or daughter. Peggy and I continued collecting cans and tin foil, and soon we added newspapers to our list of War Effort activities.

During the rest of the war, Daddy was stationed at Camp Elliott, San Diego; Camp Pendleton, Oceanside, California; and Fleet Marine Forces, Pacific. He served on the Board of Awards, Pacific Fleet. Upon Japan's surrender, he was appointed Assistant Special Services Officer, in which capacity he visited every island in the Pacific and every point in Japan, Korea, and China where a single Marine was to be found. He wrote us letters from every place he visited, but that is another story. However, there was one unforgettable letter: when his plane was landing in Nagasaki, he was shocked by the devastation and wrote us, "They must outlaw the atomic bomb."

He was then appointed as a Justice to the War Crimes Commission sitting in Guam, which dealt out penalties and acquittals to high ranking Japanese charged with atrocities in the Pacific Ocean areas. This job was followed by service as a Justice of the Supreme Court of Guam. His letters home are a testamony to his compassion and fairness.

Upon his retirement after the war, he went to law school and then practiced law until his death in 1970.

Peggy and I told our story infrequently: frankly, there were few people at home who understood us.

I feared sirens, violence and explosions.

I grew up and went to college, married, and had children. For a number of years, the exigencies of raising my children took precedence over memories. Then I began teaching. But I always had the feeling that there was a story that had to be told.

One year, a student who'd recently visited Pearl Harbor brought me a book he'd bought there. I looked at aerial photos I had never seen as well as pictures of the flaming ships I could never forget.

In June of 1982, Peggy's husband, Dean Unger, was honored as a fellow by the American Institute of Architects. The ceremony was to be held in Honolulu. Peggy, my mother, and I accompanied him. Ahead of time, I'd written Mr. Rockwell, the Naval Affairs Officer at Pearl Harbor, and he'd kindly arranged for our return to Ford Island.

We stood outside Quarters T looking, remembering. Brenda Kunkel, daughter of Captain and Mrs. Barry Kunkel, invited us inside. What joy it was to be back, to see the old familiar rooms.

After that, I corresponded with Cindy Kunkel, and she invited me and my family to the 1982 Labor Day Celebration on Ford Island. My ten year old son, Robbie, and my thirteen year old daughter, Alison, accompanied me. I wanted to see if the magic of Ford

Island and Quarters T would cast a spell over them as it had me.

It did. We three swam together in the old pool. I relived my interrupted childhood through their eyes.

I walked through the paths shaded by the trees. I traced my steps down to Kenneth Whiting School. I revisited the dungeon and heard the echo of children's voices. I looked for my mark on the now-huge old banyan tree.

At twilight I walked down to the plaque on the lawn in front the now demolished Old BOQ. I quietly observed the new view from Quarters T: the silent sentinel over a lost ship and its men, the *Arizona* Memorial. I cried. And slowly, gently, a jigsaw puzzle piece long missing from my life slid back into place.

Post Script

As my sister, Peggy, and I prepared to return to Hawaii yet again, this time for the sixtieth anniversary of the attack that so changed our lives, the unthinkable happened: September 11, 2001, and the World Trade Center/Pentagon terrorist attacks. Comparisons to it and Pearl Harbor are on everyone's minds and engraved in all our hearts: that such a travesty of trust had again occurred. I know that our nation and all its people mourn.

I also know that we will build again.

Acknowledgements

My children, John III, David, Meg, Alicia, Alison, and Robbie, who all listened to my story. My students over the years who urged me to write it down. Clive Matson, poet and teacher, who guided my first steps; Helen Harris, author and editor, who encouraged me to complete the book and facilitated its publication; my friend Gordon White for his wisdom; Oakley Hall and the Squaw Valley Community of Writers; Researchers at the National Archives, Washington D.C. and the Naval History Archives; the 14th Naval District Public Affairs Officer, Roth Rockwell, who made my first trip to Quarters T a reality and interviewed Mrs. Ulner for me; Mrs. Dorothy M. Fuller, who was Head Librarian of the Pearl Harbor Naval Base Library and supplied Naval documents and pictures; Will Hoover of the *Honolulu Advertiser* who supplied both encouragement and information; and the California Chapter of the Pearl Harbor Survivors, who understood me.

Joan Zuber Earle lived in Quarters T from November of 1940 to mid-December, 1941.

She was born in Washington D.C. while her father served at the Marine Barracks, Navy Yard, Washington D.C. She subsequently lived in Bremerton, Washington; on the Marine Base in Quantico, Virginia; in Long Beach, California; back in Quantico; in San Diego, California; on the Receiving Ship, San Francisco (Yerba Buena Island); on the Naval Air Station, Coronado, California; on the Naval Air Station, Pearl Harbor, Territory of Hawaii; in San Francisco (two different places); and then again in San Diego for her high school years. Prior to college, she attended ten different schools.

She's written all her life, from a column for the *San Diego Union* while in college, to articles in Bay Area newspapers over the years.

She received a B.A. and M.A. in History from the University of California, Berkeley. During those years, she was a member of campus honoraries Panile and Prytanean as well as of Mortar Board, a national service honorary. She was on the ASUC Executive Committee and a member of Phi Alpha Theta, History Honorary.

Her professional life has been devoted to education; she's taught since 1955. She has five different teaching credentials, elementary through Community College.

For the last thirteen years, she's been a Resource Specialist at the Fred Finch Youth Center in Oakland. It's one of the largest non-profits in the San Francisco East Bay: since 1891, this center has changed the lives of over 20,000 children -- children who have frequently been abused, neglected, and/or abandoned.

For eighteen years she's also been an Instructor for the University of California at Berkeley Extension

Online, through which she's taught students from all over the world.

She also runs a private practice, "Love of Learning," as an Educational Therapist, in which capacity she's evaluated and treated learning problems in young children, adolescents, and adults: problems such as dyslexia, attention deficit disorder, reading, writing, language, math, and deficits in self-esteem, motivation, social skills, and/or organizational and study skills. She's a member of the Association of Educational Therapists.

Her six children and five grandchildren live near her in the San Francisco Bay Area. The Piedmont home where she raised her children is reminiscent of Quarters T. It has -- yes, she counted them -- five doors out.